APR 2007

W9-BNL-098

The Night My Sister
Went Missing

OTHER NOVELS BY CAROL PLUM-UCCI

The Body of Christopher Creed

What Happened to Lani Garver

The She

CAROL PLUM-UCCI

The Night My Sister Went Missing

Harcourt, Inc.
Orlando Austin New York
San Diego Toronto London

Requests for permission to make copies of any part of the work should
be submitted online at www.harcourt.com/contact or mailed to the following
address: Permissions Department, Harcourt, Inc., 6277 Sea Harbor Drive,
Orlando, Florida 32887-6777.

www.HarcourtBooks.com

Library of Congress Cataloging-in-Publication Data
Plum-Ucci, Carol, 1957–
The night my sister went missing/Carol Plum-Ucci.
p. cm.
Summary: When his sister goes missing under mysterious circumstances,
seventeen-year-old Kurt spends a night at the local police station overhearing
statements from a variety of witnesses that reveal the deep prejudices and
shocking secrets of his small beach community.
[1. Missing children—Fiction.   2. Secrets—Fiction.   3. Incest—Fiction.
4. City and town life—Fiction.   5. Gossip—Fiction.]   I. Title.
PZ7.P7323Nig   2006
[Fic]—dc22   2005035081
ISBN-13: 978-0-15-204758-0   ISBN-10: 0-15-204758-1

Text set in Minion
Designed by Cathy Riggs

First edition
H G F E D C B A

Printed in the United States of America

This is a work of fiction. All the names, characters, organizations, and events
portrayed in this book are products of the author's imagination. Any resemblance
to any organization, event, or actual person, living or dead, is unintentional.

TO:
All of my English students.
ALL of you.
You're all NUTZ.
I love you.
You're gonna make it.

1

The night my sister went missing, I sat in a back corridor of the police station, staring at a tinted glass window to an inner room. The lights were off in there, and so the window looked like a black screen. I remember how my insides felt as blank as that window. It's a good thing, that numbness, because it keeps you from spiraling into the black-hole-falling routine. Something's telling you that you don't need those panic-stricken thoughts yet.

No body had washed up. The police hadn't found any blood on the pier near the spot where Casey went over. The gunshot, which had sounded more like a weather-wet fire-cracker, could not possibly have hit one of Casey's vital or-gans. Of course, there are always the thoughts that threaten you—like how blood in the ocean draws sharks, and how a storm at sea had created endless riptides this week. But thoughts like that bounce in the first hours after your shock.

The good thoughts strike you and stick. Like, my sister was probably a better swimmer than I was, even though I was a lifeguard. And I thought of Casey having so many friends. None of our friends had any streak of violence. No one had any reason to hurt her.

It had been too dark to see anything but a few clusters of our friends up on the pier in silhouette, and I tried hard not to put anything in my mind that wasn't real.

The gun had been real, whether I liked it or not. But it was a stupid little collector's gun, a derringer, or "lady's pistol," as my buddies called it, brought to a dune party as a joke. It all seemed surreal now. And all of it smelled of "accident." Nobody who'd sneaked up on the old pier with us would intentionally hurt Casey. Nobody.

Maybe this was all a big prank that had gone over the top. I thought of Casey painting "drops of blood" out of the cafeteria this year, and also pulling the fire alarm to relieve friends from a couple of boring classes. Maybe she was holed up on some sailboat in the back bay, laughing her airhead butt off, ignorant that the coast guard and the police were searching the ocean around the pier.

I hadn't seen or heard much in the light of a half-covered moon—except I'd still swear I heard Casey's laugh, and it was after the little *Crack!*

I'd been able to relay all that over the phone to our parents in a miraculous calm. Still, they were scrambling to catch the red-eye back from L.A., where my dad had been in film negotiations with Paramount. It was the first time one of his novels had been optioned by a movie company— and the first time our parents had left me and Casey alone overnight since we were fourteen and twelve. I was now seventeen, and I stared at that tinted glass window, seeing Dad's cockeyed grin in it and hearing his speech about how he trusted a twelve- and a fourteen-year-old home alone far more than he trusted a fifteen- and a seventeen-year-old.

He had tried to tempt us. "Come on, Kurt . . . maybe I'll strike it rich finally. You kids need to be there. And you and Casey could do Disneyland, while—"

I had stopped him right there. The "rich" part would have struck me better ten years ago, when I was *first* getting sick of peanut butter sandwiches for lunch seven days a week. By now I was immune to the midlist author no-frills life, and I started blathering about my job on the beach patrol. I probably could have got time off for a Monday through Thursday—it's weekends that are sacred for lifeguards. But my job was a good enough excuse to balk at leaving Mystic in the middle of July. The previous summer Mom and Dad had wanted to take Casey and me to the Greek isles for ten days, after my dad finally got a better-than-average royalty check. My very first thought had been, *Can we take friends?* I didn't ask. I just made excuses until they dropped the whole idea—my point being that if the Greek isles can't tempt a guy away from summer fun 'n' games, Disneyland surely isn't gonna cut it. Not that fun 'n' games is anything too awful.

I had sworn up and down, while Dad was deciding to let us stay home alone, that we wouldn't do anything stupid, and I still felt that I had held up my end of that bargain. Mostly.

All we'd done wrong was go to a dune party. My mom and dad wouldn't object to us going to a house party while they were gone. But a dune party was different. No chance of adults, good chance of a raid by the cops . . . and of course there were always the daredevils, loadies, and lovers who would risk going up on the burned-out old pier. No matter how many times the cops removed the metal climbing spikes from its scorched pilings, more would be found hammered in a week or so later.

We were all just goofing around, risking a rip-tear out on the least scorched portion of the pier's planking, because it was fun, because of the horror tales about the place, because most people were partied so loose that if a couple of them fell through and hit the waves, they probably wouldn't feel it. I guessed we'd forgotten about the storm at sea and how big the rips were.

And I guessed the partying wasn't so good, either. But millions of kids party, and hundreds of kids had climbed up on the pier in the past twenty years, weather not a consideration. Their sisters don't get shot by some dinky "lady's pistol" and fall into the surf with barely a splash. That was the weirdest. Through the deepest, darkest corners of my memory, I still kept digging for the sound of a splash. I couldn't find it.

Your numbness, your denial, might make you have a flash of Peter Pan saving Wendy from walking the plank. I conjured up images of Captain Hook and Mr. Smeed listening for the splash after Wendy walked the plank, but I couldn't find a splash after Casey fell backward.

But then, Peter Pan hadn't wandered over to the New Jersey barrier islands to catch Casey Carmody midfall off the old fishing pier. That much, you can grasp. The theory of ghosts doesn't work well either, suddenly. When my dad was a kid, the old fishing pier, which is actually pretty big, had been turned into The Haunt, an amusement pier with an enormous haunted mansion exhibit at the entrance. It had been a "megaproduction," as Dad called it, employing half the eighteen-year-olds on the island to dress up like vampires and headless ghouls and jump out at summer tourists and their kids. But The Haunt loomed on the far south end of a barrier island, with only a small toll bridge at the far north end. The island couldn't hack the traffic that The Haunt needed to survive. About twenty years ago it went bankrupt, and legend has it that some kid was under the pier lighting off firecrackers and that's how the fire started. No one really knows for sure.

It wasn't a good enough story to attract the attention of kids in high school. Sightings of vampires hovering over the burned-out foundation of the haunted house, plus two tales of the suicides off there—one in the eighties and one in the nineties—those things drew kids to the place like the moon draws water.

But island lore about "sightings of the suicide victims" and "the vampires who made them do it" didn't fit the mood in the police station, where I now found myself. Spooks are for fun in the dark. This place was lit and immaculate and stinking of floor soap, and right now, all too quiet, what with the entire police force out on the beach.

I became aware of my one shoulder being rubbed, and my eyes dropped to the knees of Cecilly Holst. Cecilly was a nice girl—usually. Put it this way: She had always been nice to me, but I'd heard her mouth in action against certain violators of her Code of Acceptable Behavior Around Here. Picture Hilary Duff, only hired to play a mean Lizzie McGuire instead of a doofus one. There were probably a thousand ways to earn Cecilly's scowling, hair-tossing wrath, but I had never done that, so that side of her didn't apply to the here and now. Her eyes were not scowling, but they were still sharp. I don't know why she kept watching me. But I sensed that if I broke down and cried or something, she would hug me and have no problem with it. I was glad to have her there.

Her best friend, True, sat on the other side of me. True's real name is Sandra Blueman, but she picked up the nickname True Blue in high school, and then simply True. True was turned toward me, her long legs pulled together nervously at the knees and her toes turned under in her flip-flops. She was stroking her endless dark ponytail and looking lost in thought, which was fine. If two girls had been rubbing me at that moment, I would have felt mauled.

"I don't know why they won't let you back down to the beach while the coast guard searches," Cecilly muttered. "You want me to talk to my dad?"

Her dad was the island psychiatrist and director of the Drug and Alcohol Rehab Clinic of Mainland Hospital. Because some of his clientele came from police arrests, he had a good relationship with the cops around here. He had enough pull with Cecilly that she didn't usually imbibe like other kids. That explained her presence here at the police station. Everyone who had been partying had steered clear of me once the cops showed up and started asking questions.

"No . . ." I rubbed my eyes hard, not that they itched. I figured the bottom line: The police didn't want me on the beach if a body suddenly bobbed up in the surf. They might let me stay there if my parents were there, too, but the flight from L.A. wouldn't get them here until at least six A.M. I looked at my watch. 11:36. I had been here for an hour, but it felt like three. "I just wish they would let me go to someone's house to wait for my folks."

"You want to come to my house?" Cecilly straightened. "I'll go call my dad. He's got his cell phone on the beach. He'll send my mom—"

"Captain Lutz told me I couldn't leave." I shrugged. "They took my cell phone, in case Casey is holed up somewhere and tries to call."

8

"A body can't go anywhere without its cell phone . . . ," Cecilly droned to be funny, and none of us laughed.

"I already told him everything I saw. Which wasn't a lot. I told them everything I heard, smelled, thought, felt, did. I don't know why I have to stay."

"You're a minor. They don't want you going off by yourself," True muttered, bouncing a loose fist off my knee. "Believe me, they don't suspect you of anything."

That thought hadn't even occurred to me. But having heard True say it, I stiffened, and my mind started spitting out recent memories. Casey and I had got into a screaming match the night before. She had just started going out with another lifeguard, Mark Stern, and she'd wanted to take him up to her bedroom to "watch TV." I was just being a big brother. Stern is a year older than me, with three years in on the beach patrol compared to my two. Not a guy you'd let up in your fifteen-year-old sister's bedroom to "watch TV," not without a loud fight. *Had the neighbors heard my yelling? Or Casey's shrill comebacks? Did Stern tell the cops that I had said, "Touch my sister, and you're both dead"? Was he down on the beach right now, making me out to be some maniac?*

Cecilly's laughter sliced through my thoughts, and I searched her sympathetic eyes. "Kurt, there were twenty people up there, all of whom would say you were nowhere near Casey, nowhere near that . . . disgusting little pistol, either. Chill down. I don't even think they'll drug-test you. Too much stress on one family if you—"

"They can drug-test me!" I said defensively. "I have not . . . done anything wrong!"

I knew that last line was less than true, and probably the only reason I was stone-cold sober was that the parents were away, and something kept eating at me to act like an adult. As much as possible. It had seemed like a sacrifice to the party gods not to have my usual two and a half beers, which is all you can have if you're a puker. At seventeen you're too old to be puking in bushes after a six-pack. Time to grow up. And I had just never smoked pot. Call me boring. Casey had, though, and I tried to remember if she'd smoked any tonight. It seemed to me the last time I looked at her, maybe five minutes before the little pistol crack, I had seen her with something lit, but I thought it was her biweekly cigarette-at-a-party.

I had been on the other side of the pier, talking to, of all people, Billy Nast, science gleep extraordinaire. I still hadn't figured out who had brought him to this party. But I'd latched on to his talk about just having finished a month at Purdue, and these summer engineering courses he'd actually taken there. Girls kept coming up and doing that thing with their knees, trying to collapse my knees from behind— their way of telling me I was acting very strange. But I hadn't wanted to leave Nast alone in a crowd that was drinking and could potentially get, um, pointed.

And besides, I'd been having secret qualms about the Naval Academy. My getting accepted there had made me famous around Mystic. Between my parents, relatives, teachers, coaches, and the newspapers, I didn't feel I could think aloud to anyone about my qualms—and I wasn't even sure why I would pick such a time to start dwelling on nauseating concepts such as "killing people for a living." All I'd thought about for two years before the acceptance letter arrived was getting in. So I felt a little whacked out, like, wondering if I was schizoid, or if there is a devil that likes to embarrass you. Anyway, there was Billy Nast, talking enthusiastically about becoming an astronaut, giving alternatives in case I totally needed one.

I'd been hypnotized, not only by his enthusiasm for taking college classes during the summer but also with the thought that he really wasn't all that gleepy. I sat there listening to him, wondering, *What is a gleep, anyway? What does that mean?*

That was all before Casey fell. Afterward I wanted to throttle him. If I'd been doing the same old fooling around with the same old friends, maybe I could have been closer to Casey. Maybe I could have grabbed her arm. Maybe I would have seen whether this blood-rushing-through-her-fingers thing was truth or moonlight. I knew it was stupid to blame Billy Nast, and I tried not to. But the bottom line was, I hadn't been close at all, hadn't even heard Casey hit the water in the long, wily, unforgettable silence before people started screaming.

"Why do people party?" I asked Cecily and True. I wanted to blame someone, though it was too soon to blame individuals, so society in general seemed appropriate.

They said nothing. Some questions aren't worth trying to answer.

"We'll straighten the cops out." Cecilly rubbed my back some more, though her normally dead-on gaze dropped a little. "Huh, True?"

"Yeah. Don't worry about anything, Kurt."

Their lowered eyes spoke volumes, yet no way was I ready to start filling in the void. Missing from it was the ever-important question: *What did you guys see?* Their tones implied they had seen a lot. Their tones implied what they'd seen was not good—if an accident, a stupid one; a gun had been fired, and someone ought to go to jail for attempted manslaughter, at least. Their tones said they were prepared to tell the truth to the cops.

I appreciated that, as well as the fact that they weren't sitting here spewing the details into my face yet. You would think that if your sister fell off a pier after a gun had been fired, you would want every little morsel of information, and as quickly as possible. But there are times you really feel like you need the police or some adult company to give you some adult wisdom, or you might wind up going crazy.

I felt a slight breeze run over me and looked down the long corridor. The double doors were not visible from way back here where Captain Lutz had sat me down, but I knew they had opened. I walked out there, and True and Cecilly followed. Lutz came toward us with sand all over his shoes. The cuffs of his uniform trousers were wet and sandy, also.

"Nothing yet. Hang steady." He put his hands on his hips and watched me breathlessly. I searched his eyes for some sort of judgment, some I-told-you-so glare, because, in school and out, he was always blowing smoke about kids on the pier. But he looked distracted by other things, including Cecilly and True being on either side of me. His eyes bounced back and forth.

"You girls want to give a statement?"

"Yes."

"Yes."

There was nervousness in both voices, as if they sensed they were breaking some code of ethics. I didn't exactly fault all the kids who ran. I was too numb to fault anyone yet, but I was slightly agog that even a pistol crack and someone falling wouldn't stop some of those people from their usual flight syndrome when the cops show up. I would think of that later. For now I was glad for these two.

Lutz gestured them to come with him to his office, a little farther down the hall, and he sounded grateful, if tense. "Great. There's two I won't have to round up. Kurt, wait out here. You girls can start filling out the statement form, and then I'll see you one at a time."

I watched him shut the door to the back offices, which were just cubicles in a big room. It wasn't big as police stations go.

Mystic, like most barrier islands, is pencil shaped and hugs the coast. It's seven miles long, but only the three-mile middle section is wide enough to be inhabitable. Even there, every ten years or so, a northeast storm at full moon will send the ocean to meet the bay in the middle of Central Avenue. Water will run like a river up Bay Drive and Ocean Drive, which is why most of the island houses are built with nothing but concrete garages and a rec room on the first floor. Nearly every house has a waterline stain around the outside of the garage.

Total inhabitants: three thousand in the winter, eighteen thousand in the summer.

Usually in July someone would bring some summer person around to hang with us. We were nice and all, but the person rarely came back, sensing, I think, that life was established around here. We knew one another, one another's families, and we knew the islanders who would qualify as family because we'd seen them regularly on the street since we were born.

I suspected Lutz would find out who was on the pier and round up all twenty or so of the Mystic Marvels who had been present. That's what we called our clan around school—the Mystic Marvels. Casey had actually dreamed up that term last year as a freshmen and it kind of went everywhere and stuck. There were maybe five kids who were freshmen and a dozen kids in each of the sophomore, junior, and senior classes who seemed to qualify as Mystic Marvels—not too bad, not too good, not too smart, not too dumb, not too rich, not too poor, just "marvy all around," as Casey loved to say. We had a bad reputation with the too-smarts and too-goods. We were loathed by the too-bads, but we figured some people are just jealous. Because the island only has one block of slum at the far south end, the too-poors are all but nonexistent, and the too-riches are usually summer people, who don't count as islanders.

We had our almost-riches, as my dad smilingly called them, which would include whatever types could make a decent living in an area that has no industry: doctors, lawyers, insurance salesmen, and because there was so much waterfront property, real estate agents. A lot of their kids were among my friends, but we melted in with some people like True, too, no questions asked. Her dad was the pastor of Mystic Baptist Church, and the family lived on church-basket collections. Casey and I are accepted, though my dad never ceased to remind me that midlist authors don't qualify as almost-riches. He says that because of his job, we're "novel" and can go anywhere. Hardy-har.

That's life around here. Because of it, Cecilly and True couldn't technically be accused of busting anyone if they gave names. The cops could drive up and down the streets, stopping at each house and asking to speak to so-and-so, like newspaper chuckers who have memorized a paper route.

I let myself spiral a little as the aloneness sent waves of panic into my gut. The minutes passing weighed on me, reminding me that it only takes four minutes to drown. This was not good, *not good*, and the thought drew a mouthful of spit I was forced to swallow. I jerked my head and focused on the end of the corridor. A presence filled the doorway. I all but bounced to my feet seeing Drew Aikerman.

It wasn't Casey, but my best friend was all right, and I did what I had never done before. I dropped my head into his shoulder and didn't make any bullshit joke when his arms went around me. His hair was still wet, and a layer of beach sand found its way into my eyes and teeth—another thing that spoke volumes. Drew was a lifeguard, too, which maybe made him useful to the coast guard. He'd searched the tide with them until he'd probably collapsed in the sand before making his way here.

"Went to your house first, since all your lights were on," he said. It was an apology for not getting here sooner.

"I kept telling Casey to turn off the lights," I muttered, backing up. "She's so . . . airy." I felt a tinge of guilt, cutting on her right now, but it made everything seem a little more normal.

Drew just looked me in the eye. "I think she's holed up in the back bay. Let's face it. She's a good swimmer, fantastic diver. And it would be like her to, you know . . ." He left the sentence dangling, as if it might go against his normal politeness to say, "pull a fast one on us."

I didn't say anything, but the definition of "good swimmer, fantastic diver" gripped at me. You could fit a three-story house under the pilings at the end of the pier. And Casey had been wearing my new Naval Academy sweatshirt that, soaked in water, would have weighed her down if she'd hit the water wrong and injured herself. She'd have been blatantly stupid to dive off that pier and risk her neck—then risk trying to stay afloat in my sweatshirt.

Just two years ago Casey had broken her neck in a fluke accident on water skis. You'd think after being in a halo for two months that she would never take another dare, never risk a dangerous prank. I hadn't seen Casey "risk her neck" for a prank since then, but she *had* gone back to mountain climbing, ski jumping, and was already cocaptain of the diving team at school, in spite of my mom being ripped up about it. Casey's cracked vertebra healed completely, but Mom says it's her carelessness that puts her in danger, not her skeletal system. Casey, of course, says she's not careless, and besides, swimmers are a dime a dozen but divers are hard to find. The scholarship money is awesome.

If she isn't outright careless, Casey loves to test the limits. She had talked a blue streak last summer about wanting to take a dive off the end of that pier. She'd spent many a dune party telling us that the water was at least forty feet deep at high tide, and that someday she would do it. But there were things to consider, like the halo, the scholarships at risk, and surfers who say the thrust of the surf around the pilings is like the Perfect Storm. The shelled-out remains of the pier vibrate when the surf is up. It had been up tonight. You just have to believe my sister would not be that much of a lunatic.

I sat across from Drew, staring at the hallway tiles under our bare feet.

"It's not time to worry yet," he said.

I looked over his wet sandiness. "Thanks. For everything."

"Don't be stupid. Cops still won't let you down there?"

"No."

"How did I guess that?" Sarcasm bounced through his voice. His dad was chief of police, so Drew was the cop behavior expert. He sat in a chair beside me and leaned his elbows on his knees. He fidgeted about six times before saying, "Um . . . I didn't see it happen."

"Me neither. I basically just heard it."

"I thought it was a firecracker."

"Me, too. I was talking it up with Billy Nast, of all people. How the hell did he get there?"

"Um . . ." Drew raised his hand guiltily. "I was trying to help us out. You know, with that thing we've been talking about."

"What, our boredom thing?"

He nodded. "I knew exactly what you were talking about the other night when you said you felt all hemmed in, and you were suddenly 'seeing most of our friends in black-and-white.' That was profound."

I shifted uncomfortably. Drew and I would get to shooting the bull, but half the time I couldn't remember having said the things he quoted back at me. It's weird, having your best friend find you profound half the time.

"In fact, I took that one to *Madame School Teachaire*," he said, which was his pet name for his mom, who teaches freshman English. "I said, 'Mom, Kurt and I are seeing our friends in black-and-white. What's up with that?' She knew right away what I meant. She said that's normal. We're seniors. We're supposed to want to branch out, try a few new flavors. I saw Nast out on the fishing jetty this morning, just sitting there—without a fishing pole—like some dork. I dunno, it's like you said. Something sucked me toward him, and I just started talking to him. He wasn't *that* weird. To throw a Billy Nast type into a party, that isn't such a crime."

I sighed. "Tell that to the, um, ladies."

Drew bit on his lip and stared at the floor—enough time spent on small talk. "So . . . you do know that was a real pistol. It wasn't a toy."

I nodded, swallowing. "Jeezus and Mary. This is the type of stuff you read about in a newspaper from, like, Omaha. Do me a favor. Don't tell me who was stupid enough to . . . to own a real pistol, let alone bring it to a party. Sorry, I'm just not ready to be that angry yet."

"Okay."

"For one thing, first I have to get over being pissed at myself. I had the thing in my hand."

"So did everybody."

"It looked like a goddamned toy, Drew."

"That was the bottom line . . . the stupid pill. Mark Stern passed it to me, and he said, 'Check this out. It's *not* a toy.' I mean, if he had said, 'This is a toy,' wouldn't you have been, like, '*So?*' We wanted to touch it because it *wasn't* a toy."

I thought of my hand going around that little thing. I could almost close my fist around it—that's how small it was. If it had been some giant Luger, I would have been shouting, "What the fuck, moron! Get that thing away from us!" I might have secretly busted the person to Drew's dad—but then, a big gun like that would not have ended up at a party with us. The size, the almost-toy factor made it look so . . . *holdable.* I had thought about holding it the right way—putting my finger on the trigger. It really had been tempting. But some things you just don't do. At least not when you're stone-cold sober. Some airhead hadn't been able to resist temptation, obviously.

"I don't want to know who was holding that thing when it went off, Drew."

"Well, I don't know that, anyway. I've heard five or six versions of the trail of hands it passed through. I don't know what to believe. I only know who owned it."

"I don't want to know yet."

"Okay." He blew air into his cheeks, puffing them out while staring at the floor.

With him acting like Mount Vesuvius, I plopped down, gripped the bottom of the chair, shut my eyes tight, and braced myself. "Oh, for god's sake . . . Just tell me."

I'd actually been hoping it was Mark Stern and I could get him put away, at least for possession of a deadly weapon. Eighteen-year-olds have no business going out with fifteen-year-olds, especially when the fifteen-year-old is your sister. And he had become what I call a fringe dweller of the

Mystic Marvels. In high school he'd been great—football and basketball starter, party comedian extraordinaire. But lately girls had started to call him sleazy, because he'd now had four girlfriends in our crowd. He hung with us every weekend like he was still in high school, and I was hearing drug rumors lately, too. Let's say he was on my nerves before he started in with my sister.

"Stacy Kearney owns it," Drew said.

I sat back, watching his eyes, wondering if he actually believed that, wondering if I should or I shouldn't.

"'Stacy Kearney.'" I repeated this morsel.

I watched Drew for a long time. Of course Stacy Kearney would stand as prime suspect if any tragedy actually happened on this island. What with feeling so restless lately, and like the Technicolor in my friends was fading slowly down to dusty gray, the suggestion left me a little defensive and insulted—like you might feel after guessing the end of a made-for-TV drama.

2

Stacy Kearney. I'm trying to think up a title that would fit a girl like this, though the best I can probably come up with is the Fallen Queen type. I had seen her "fall" and had never been sure I approved of what was happening to her or not. She was a year younger than me but so noticeable that I knew her name on the first day of school my sophomore year. She was *too* perfect. Too blond, too outgoing and fun, a little too sure of herself for anyone to mess with. She fell into our crowd like she had one foot on a banana peel— despite having just moved here from Connecticut, like, two days before school started.

It takes a special talent, penetrating a crowd that included girls who, if not exactly vicious, weren't looking to play Welcome Wagon. It also was probably interesting to some people that she had the name DeWinter in her family.

Her mom's parents were DeWinters, and the DeWinters had owned almost all of Mystic, like, two generations back. Stacy's DeWinter grandparents still owned the last nine vacant lots on the island, and their house was in the dead center of town, taking up, like, half a block. If you know anything about beach houses, they're usually so smooshed in together, you can water your lawn just with a garden hose. I knew about how much money the DeWinters gave away to various causes, because my dad was a recipient: the DeWinter Grant for Artists with a Work-in-Progress. Ten thousand smackers, two years in a row. Dad would get those grants, and for at least a month I'd have cold cuts instead of peanut butter for lunch.

But I think most kids were drawn to Stacy for the more likely reasons. Pools, believe it or not, are a novelty to islanders. The DeWinters had a huge pool and a tennis court, and one of the few houses on the island that actually boasts a basement. The basement was finished and made for awesome parties, especially since the grandparents were getting too arthritic to come down the stairs.

I guess you could say Stacy seemed like the type of person you'd love to hate—except for the fact that her house was so supercharged with problems. Everyone knew about Stacy's mom and dad, and that itself probably kept people's jealousy buttons from getting pushed. Mrs. Kearney was known as the island "fling," and she was also rumored to be addicted to pain medication. Kids said that Mr. Kearney looked, smelled, and talked sort of like a lawn mower. We said that probably because he had this little lawn service—he'd been cutting people's grass since he got out of high school. That was how the two of them met. Stacy's mom, the heir to the DeWinter fortune, took off to Connecticut with the guy who mowed their grass. It was a snicker-fest scandal that died way down about the time I was born. But it came back to life again with a vengeance when the Kearneys finally moved in with the DeWinters, when Stacy was fourteen. Due to all of this, I'd say it was hard for anyone to envy Stacy. I guess most people's parents are seen as embarrassing, but it's for acting goofy—not for being a sleaze bucket and a slob.

Stacy acted like neither of her parents existed, but you could tell if you knew her well enough that she could swelter in her own little hells. At least, I could see it. Maybe it was because of my dad, Mr. Insight, always prompting me: "The girl's probably confused about people and things she's got no control over. Be nice to her."

Being nice hadn't been too much of a problem. For two years she was one of those people you'd consider the life of the party.

Then this year a lot of girls in our crowd were suddenly bashing on her—or maybe *bashing* is the wrong word. They were rolling their eyes, rehashing this or that story about how mean Stacy had gotten. She still hung out with us, though it seemed like maybe half the time instead of all the time. Her best friend, Alisa Cox, still stuck up for her when any of these stories rolled her way. She would bat her eyelashes in the sarcastic way only Alisa Cox could do, and say, "Stacy's like your average rock star: First, the public needs to build her up. Then, they need to knock her down."

The girls in our crowd could be thoughtless for sure, but they weren't evil people. I guess the stories being told about Stacy didn't seem worth the reaction that was forming, if that makes sense. The charges from the girls were hazy, things like, "She's just too much of a bitch. I can't hack it anymore."

"Stacy Kearney," I repeated again, and Drew lowered his head, drumming on his legs with his fingers.

"Yeah, yeah. I know. You're thinking that's more, um . . . bitch speculation."

"It's awfully convenient." I squirmed under the concept of a made-for-TV ending. "These girls all decide they hate her, and suddenly she owns this pistol."

"Well, unfortunately, I heard she was the owner before it went off. Back when everybody still thought it was funny. You know how people are. They'd get it in their hands, and the first question would be, of course, 'Is it loaded?' Unfortunately, the answer was wrong. The second question would be, 'Whose is it?' When I asked it, Cecilly Holst answered: 'It's Stacy Kearney's.'"

I swallowed. Cecilly and Stacy were often pretty tense around each other, and they'd been dubbed by more insightful kids in our crowd as "too much alike." They were both highly opinionated, vocal, stubborn, never backing down from an argument. I always felt sorry for girls in one of the quieter crowds if they somehow earned the shared wrath of these two. People who didn't hang with us were under the mistaken idea that Stacy and Cecilly were best friends. It was only those of us closest to them who saw that Cecilly and True were really best friends, and that Stacy and Alisa were, too. True and Alisa were quieter, and Stacy and Cecilly could light up a room.

I'd seen Stacy and Cecilly go as much as a couple of weeks without speaking to each other. Then one day they'd be hugging each other, and saying they were sorry and how much they loved each other. It was hills and valleys with those two.

I looked down at my thumbnail, seeing past it. "Tell me something. Did Stacy ever get in your face?"

"No," Drew said, rubbing the back of his neck and yawning. "I saw her lay a few girls to waste. Glad I'm not a girl. Why? She ever rip into you?"

I smiled just a little, wondering if I should just take off my watch. The temptation to keep looking at it made it weigh a hundred pounds.

"Not really." I dropped my wrist between my knees and forced myself to look away. "Well, once she did, but she apologized right after. About six weeks ago."

"What did she say?"

"It was a school night. I was walking home from baseball by myself, for once. She was coming up Central Avenue with three huge pillowcases full of what looked like wash. I had to do the Coin-Op routine with Mom once when our washer broke, so I sympathized. I just tried to take one of the pillowcases to help her carry it in. She utterly jumped on me, all, 'Do I look crippled? Aren't you a little old to be a Boy Scout?'"

Drew shuddered. "Why does she get like that sometimes? It's so not PC to talk about girls and PMS, but sometimes I think the best thing we could get for her is a gift certificate to her GYN."

I shrugged. "It helps me, having a sister. I've got thick skin after Casey pulling that routine on me for years. I just muttered some, 'No, you don't look crippled, but you don't look like an octopus, either.' She let me help her. When we got inside she started apologizing, saying their washing machine had died, and everything she owned was dirty, and how annoying that was, blah-blah. She looked really sorry and tried, in her . . . subtle way, to be nice for the next few days. I just forgot about it."

"She's like Eve White and Eve Black." Drew shuddered. "Or what's that saying about the little girl? 'And when she was good, she was very, very good, but when she was bad—'"

"You gotta look at the circumstances," I said, responding from my gut. "The Coin-Op is hot and grimy. It smells. Your clothes come out wrinkled, and in the summer it's full of French Canadian tourists who all but dangle their thongs off the end of your nose. I was ready to bark at someone by the time we left."

"Yeah, but she was just going in, not coming out."

I watched him, thinking, *Let's not nitpick.*

He finally smiled a little. "Believe me, I'm not trying to catch let's-crucify-Stacy disease. I can't find a really good reason for the girls to be acting the way they're acting. But I'm not a gossip hag, either. I don't go around asking questions about stuff like that. Still, I say, 'Where there's smoke, there's fire.'"

I didn't answer, and after checking my watch a couple more times, the room behind the gray glass turned suddenly bright. Captain Lutz and Cecilly Holst moved in there and took seats at the end of a conference table.

Drew froze as Lutz's voice blared, "Just have a seat right there. I'll be with you in a minute."

Drew blinked his tired eyes at me with some sort of amused confusion on his face. "Hel-*lo*?" he said at the ceiling, but neither silhouette in the inner room responded. He snorted out a laugh. "I'm not sure we're supposed to be hearing them. I'm not sure he remembers you're out here."

I didn't care. I was just freaked that he had moved into this little room, anyway. "What, he's going to question them in *there*? This is about a stupid accident; it's not an episode of *NYPD Blue*."

"Simmer," Drew muttered. "Dad has said they added on this room because it's the state law now. You can no longer treat police statements like technology doesn't exist. They call it the questioning room. Whatever she says, Lutz will automatically tape it, too. He'll take notes, probably to keep from reminding her of the tape, but there will be a tape if he needs it."

"You're kidding," I said.

"Don't take it personally. I mean . . . not entirely. He's not exactly asking her about some crabber's traps being emptied by poachers. There was a gun and . . . If your sister dove off that pier as a joke, well, it's getting to be not funny."

"I don't like this," I stammered. "This is my podunk island, and people don't give secret testimonies in some 'questioning room.'"

"Yeah, you're from a place that will send every cop on the force down to the beach and leave nobody here to remind the police captain of who's sitting where, when he's busy focusing on technology that's probably over his head. Count your blessings, dude. It's your podunk island that could allow you to hear some of this. If you shut up and stay cool."

I wanted to shout, *My sister is a great diver! She's an airhead, but a great practical joker!* And then, *The gun was a toy!* You can almost believe what you know is not true when you really have to.

3

When Drew stuck his nose almost right up to the tinted glass without drawing any attention, I did it, too. The silhouettes cleared into perfect facial expressions, but in an odd reddish lighting. At times the whites of Cecilly's eyes seemed to glow.

"We *all* held it." Cecilly's voice floated gracefully through speakers, even though she leaned far sideways and bounced up like she had pretended to faint. "I'm sorry! Can I blame Eddie Van Doren's ghost? Or Kenny Fife's? The spooks made me do it."

Van Doren and Fife were the pier's two infamous suicides. Fife jumped in the eighties, and Van Doren blew his brains out up there four years ago. Lutz had transferred here after being a captain on the Atlantic City police force for years, because Mystic was supposed to be zero stress in

30

comparison. The night Van Doren died had been his first
night on the job.

He only glared.

"No? Okay . . . I just don't know what to say, then. True
handed it to me, saying it wasn't a toy, and it looked so
tiny . . . And True is an angel! And Drew Aikerman handed
it to her, and how good is he? You would have done the
same thing, Captain Lutz!"

He still didn't move.

"No. Okay . . ."

Drew bounced his forehead off the glass, then pretended to slit his throat. "I'm dead. Police chief's kid.
My dad'll make sure I get six times more community service than anyone else for holding a lethal weapon—" He
stopped, suddenly remembering, I guess, that community
service wasn't the most important issue here. Casey was.
I just nodded, not begrudging him his own little denial
dances.

"Even good kids do stupid things. We'll have to worry
about all that later," Lutz finally said. "Right now, I'm trying
to figure out what we have. A fall, a gunshot wound, a practical joke, or, well, I hate to say a fatality at this point, but—"

"Fire away. I'll answer anything you want. However
many times you want."

"Starting from the top."

I watched Cecilly's head dip again. "Well, we went up
onto the pier with the climbing mounts. You know . . ."

"Belonging to?"

She dipped to the side again in a pretend faint over her behavior. "Are you sure none of what I tell you leaves this room with my name attached? That shouldn't be my just reward for helping out."

"You'd be amazed at who says what behind closed doors, Cecilly. My guess is if you tell the truth, I will get basically the same story from a dozen people or more."

"Seriously?"

"Absolutely. Most people are good enough to want to help. Minus the publicity."

She dropped her hand from her forehead. "They belonged to Todd Barnes. I guess that's no secret, since you caught him last summer."

"Guess a fine wasn't enough deterrent." He jotted something down. "So you climbed up."

"Yeah, about ten of us went up at once. Another dozen or so straggled up within the next hour. Five of us were sitting by that old burned-out Saltwater Taffy Shoppe, talking about the ghost of Eddie Van Doren firing off his suicide gun every once in a while. You know that story, right? You walk down the beach at eleven-o-five, and you hear it?"

"I live here."

"Well, I'm not saying I ever believed any of that. In fact, the suicide stories are getting so overtold. The whole pier routine is getting old." She shifted around. "I think that's why I touched the stupid pistol. If life weren't so boring all of a sudden, something new like that—like a gun—oh, lord."

"Where'd the gun come from?"

"Let me see . . ." Cecilly did some twirly thing with her finger. "Mark Stern came up and handed it to Todd Barnes. Mark said, 'Check this out. Would you believe me if I told you this isn't a toy?' So Todd took it. Then Drew Aikerman took it. He asked, 'Is it loaded?' Mark said it wasn't. *Ha!* Drew passed it off really quick, you know, I guess realizing his dad was chief of police and this wasn't smart."

I remembered that Mark Stern had also told me it wasn't loaded. Still, I'd been too skittish to touch the trigger. Somebody hadn't been.

"So then True finally took it, and it came around to me, and everyone else had touched it, so . . ."

"So you held it. Then what?"

"I asked who it belonged to. Mark said it belonged to Stacy."

"Where was Stacy?"

"Looking over the north side of the pier with Alisa Cox. They were doing the old best-friend routine, putting their heads together and acting like the secret of the universe was passing between them."

"They were talking about this gun?"

"I don't think so. Alisa was rubbing the back of Stacy's head.

"They each had complicated guy problems, and Alisa had—" Cecilly snapped her fingers by her ear, like she was looking for words. "—blurted some gossip that just made it even more complicated. Alisa had just broken up with Todd

Barnes. Todd was sitting there with us, not twenty feet away. Stacy had just broken up with Mark Stern, about three weeks ago. But she was trying really hard to stay friends with him. That's why I didn't give the gun right back to Mark. Stacy had called him over, and the three of them started to talk about something."

"About this gun?"

"No, no. I really don't think Stacy was thinking about this gun one way or the other. It's almost like . . . I'm not sure she knew it was being passed around."

"Well, if she's the owner, how could she not know—"

"I guess I would have expected her to keep an eye on a thing like that if she knew it was going around. Maybe Mark got ahold of it somehow without her knowing it. They were definitely talking about something else. I heard a couple more words float over when I was waiting for Mark so that I could give the gun back."

"What words?"

"'*Nasty ass.*' Alisa was saying it, and that's, um, a nickname for Billy Nast. He was on the pier. Somehow. He doesn't hang with us very much. So I think they were talking about Billy Nast and how Kurt Carmody was spending his whole night over by the old arcade, talking to a science nerd instead of to us. Stacy didn't like it."

"Stacy did the name-calling?"

"No, Alisa did. But she's a good friend like that. Stacy's had it bad for Kurt Carmody for a while."

My neck snapped in surprise.

Lutz asked, "Stacy owns the gun, and she has a crush on the brother of the missing girl? The girl who we think was shot?" I couldn't sense where he was going with his question.

"Yeah. I guess it looks at first like there's no good reason for Stacy Kearney to point a pistol at Casey Carmody and pull the trigger. That's not the way to catch the boy of your dreams!" Cecilly laughed, sort of in confusion.

Lutz wrote some notes down.

"Stacy's probably had a crush on Kurt since forever. But she never acted on it. She'd always say things to me like, 'He's too nice. I'd ruin him.' She loved to joke about her own bitchiness, but I think she halfway believed it, because she never came on to Kurt. She'd go out with, um, people of lesser value? Does that sound horrible? It's not exactly that they were *less* valuable. It's just that Kurt is *more* valuable. He's pretty special to everyone."

Drew patted me on the head silently, and I pulled away, embarrassed. This wasn't the first time I'd heard myself referred to as something very good—either fair or honest or happy or a noncomplainer—though it seemed to me that I could bust down as easily as the next person. I just lived with thoughts that nobody needs to hear me whine, or nobody needs to be bothered with my problems. I kept most things to myself, or wrote things down in this ever-growing blog board.

I had blogged my ass off this summer. It started with wanting to think about why the Naval Academy suddenly felt all wrong for me, but I wrote about other things, too. I wrote about how this spring I'd started seeing all my friends in black-and-white, and other bloggers had different ways of posting the same thing.

The stories that people responded to the most were my descriptions of "black breezes" and the ghosts up on the pier. A black breeze is a term I made up for what had been happening to me at dune parties or on the pier when we sneaked up there. It's the feeling like someone has walked up behind you and is breathing right onto your neck. But when you spin, nobody is there.

Lots of people who posted either had a story about when they'd had a black breeze, or they wanted to ask questions about the suicides. Chatting online ended up distracting me from my Naval Academy woes more than solving them for me. But blogging was getting to be an addiction. Like, I knew I would have to blog this whole thing about my sister being missing at some point, even though I didn't know how it would end yet. I couldn't think about the ending. But I started, like, compulsively thinking through the strange parts that I knew already.

The first strange thing I'd have to blog was that I'd had about the worst black breeze ever maybe five minutes before Casey fell. I had been listening to Billy Nast, and I just kept listening. I didn't want Nast thinking I was nuts, so for once I hadn't spun around. Now I wished I had. I might have seen something—not a spook or anything, because I don't know how much I actually believe in my own black breezes. I might have seen where the shot had come from. I might have seen who had the gun.

The second strange thing I'd have to blog was the weirdness of not hearing any splash. The last thing would have to be what I'd just heard: *Stacy Kearney likes me.*

Stacy had always seemed to me—to use really dangerous terminology—like a gun ready to go off. As fun as she could be, I could never get comfortable around her, because there was always this underlying . . . jumpiness. I'd come away from her feeling tied up in knots, even if she had been totally cool. I would not have gone out with her, though I also thought Cecilly was taking Stacy way too seriously. If a girl liked me, I knew it. It shows, no matter how hard they try to hide it.

Lutz finally quit writing. "So Mark left your circle of friends to talk to Stacy. What did you do with the gun?"

"If you can believe this, I passed the gun to Casey Carmody," Cecilly said, slumping sideways yet again.

"But you're sure she wasn't holding it when it went off?"

"I'm positive. She's a little . . . well, some people call her an airhead. I just think she's a daredevil. She loves danger and doesn't stop to think sometimes. Remember when she tried to do her flip on water skis, what, two years back?"

"A day that has lived in infamy around here," he muttered. "Being that she spent all of August and September in a halo, I'm highly doubtful that she would be fool enough to dive off the pier."

Cecilly squirmed around in her seat. "No? Tonight she actually held the gun the right way, with her finger on the trigger, and started swinging it around."

I flinched. *Leave it to Casey.*

He wrote some more. "And then?"

"I yelled at her for doing that, and she just cupped it in her hand after that. I went to find Mark but got distracted. About five minutes later, I went back to look for her, though. I mean . . . just to make sure she wasn't doing anything stupid with it. But she said she gave it to . . . somebody else— I can't remember, but she said that person gave it back to Mark Stern."

"Who gave it to me," I murmured, and Drew looked at me. "You know what? I asked Billy Nast if he wanted to hold it. He laughed and said, 'No, thanks,' and just kept on talking."

Drew lay his head on his hand. "Science dork! Maybe we should have been science dorks. Why didn't I get pissed and hurl the damn thing over the side?"

Somebody had hurled it. The damn thing was nowhere to be found since Casey fell. But I wished it had been me, so now I wouldn't look so stupid and Nast so smart.

I'd always felt secretly that the science dorks had an easier life, though it was hard to put my finger on why. They seemed less pressured, at least socially. It struck me that their friends were probably less judgmental. They could relax more, because they could mess up more. I remembered how close I had come to telling Billy Nast that I was strung out about the Naval Academy, and how weird that urge had seemed since I hadn't told any of my friends.

I had fifteen or so blog slogs answer me to quit the whole damn Naval Academy thing now, before it was too late—before I snapped, midsemester, and had to leave in disgrace or something. I was still at the point of trying to decide if they were really posting what would be in my best interest, or if they were telling me this because none of them was going to a school I had even heard of. My dad, who's full of sayings, has one that's appropriate: "People love to see you get ahead—so long as you don't get farther ahead than they are." But you can't post that without sounding arrogant instead of confused and embarrassed. Billy Nast had started to feel like my first real alternate sounding board. Then all this trouble happened.

I looked back at Cecilly, who seemed to be getting down to something important finally, because she was going off again about confidentiality. ". . . seriously. I *will* help. But I don't want to lose all my friends because of it. I don't want to play the true confessor on Mystic—"

"Um, let's keep in mind the potential seriousness of this," Lutz interrupted, making his voice louder than hers.

". . . Stacy just broke up with Mark Stern three weeks ago, but last week—*surprise!*—he started going out with Casey Carmody."

Lutz wrote that down.

"And tonight, a few of us found out something. Stacy is pregnant."

I turned my head slowly to look at Drew. His jaw hung, like I suppose mine did, confirming that he hadn't heard this, either. Lutz kept writing. I sensed he was trying to get ahold of himself and stay calm. "Mark Stern is the father?"

"Obviously. She just found out last week, but she's about two months along. They went out since January."

He wrote and wrote.

"So . . . what are you saying about how this relates to the gun?" Lutz finally looked up.

"Just that . . . maybe she couldn't stand the sight of him with Casey." They watched each other, and I could sense Lutz trying to appear blank.

"And let's face it," she went on. "Stacy bought a gun. I mean, that is a very weird thing for someone around here to do. I mean . . . her sense of humor is out of hand, any-way. We all know that, right?"

"But have you ever known her to be, uh, aggressive? Or violent?"

"I would say she's a bit . . . *vicious*. I've been the victim, many times. It's not just the quiet kids. But, like . . . okay." She snapped her fingers and held up her pointer. "I was with her on the last day of school in the cafeteria. She was in one of her moods from hell, and when we were walking past the chem-lab table—you know what that is?"

"I would imagine the . . . science nerds?"

"Two points. This one kid, Gary McDermott, was staring at her. I mean a lot of people stare at Stacy and me, but she doesn't take to it the way I do. I just think, *Okay, somebody thinks we look hot. That's a good thing.* For some reason she can't stand it. So she, like, barks to McDermott, 'What the hell are you looking at, McDumbnuts?' Something like that. I was all, 'Stacy. Chill out. He's a sweet kid, and all he did was look at you. It's a compliment.' Anyway, she's vicious like that."

I looked at Drew in confusion. Drew and I had been sitting at the next table, and Stacy and Cecilly were coming to us, so I was watching as that thing happened. Cecilly hadn't said anything in defense of Gary McDermott. She had just looked at him and laughed.

It was no big deal, Cecilly's memory loss; I guessed anyone could miss a fine detail. By the time they had got to me and Drew, they were their usual fun selves again, fussing with my hair, telling me I needed to buzz it this summer in prep for the academy.

"Hey. I remember Stacy trying to give you her Dunkin' Donuts bag that morning. Remember that?" Drew said.

That was right after the hair fuss. "Yeah. Had a lemon doughnut in it."

"She said that after she bought it she decided she wasn't hungry. Maybe she had morning sickness."

I nodded but searched my memory for any signs of her not feeling good. She had been almost perky, what with the McDumbnuts thing behind her. She was still a friend, and

I hated to think of her going around school all queasy and confused, maybe suspecting the worst and not knowing what to do.

"So you've noticed changes in Stacy's behavior since . . . when?" Lutz went on.

"I would say . . . since maybe April. I was actually expecting her to get a little crazy in January when her parents finally split up. But she came through that with barely a shrug. All she ever said was, 'It's about time, ey?' I didn't notice anything until months later. We used to joke with her sometimes that in a past life she was a rottweiler. It seemed like we got to saying it every day by the time school ended. And that was the week she broke up with Mark."

"*She* broke up with *him*?"

"Well, she *says* she broke up with him."

"But you have reason to believe otherwise? That he might have broken her heart?"

"Yeah. Truthfully, we'd been telling *Mark* to break up with *her*."

"Why?"

She shook her head slowly a few times. "You can put up with meanness in your friends, so long as it's not, you know, directed at any of you. If it starts coming your way too much? That is not a friend. We were starting to think even Mark Stern could do better."

"She was spiraling."

"Yeah. Lately she's been getting totally blue, flying off the handle. One minute she'll be her fun, laughing self, and the next minute she'll be snapping at you. A couple days ago a bunch of us were on the beach, and I turned the channel on her radio. She was all, *'I was listening to that song, bitch!'* I didn't get too upset about the 'bitch' part. She called everybody bitch. She'd just wander up in the mornings at school sometimes, all, 'Hey, bitch. Wha's up?'"

"That's her . . . usual greeting."

"We're used to it. It's, like, something she brought here from her 'old neighborhood.' Her grandparents might be loaded, but her life was not like this before she moved from Connecticut. She's just—" Cecilly broke off for a confused giggle. "—just this odd combination of too rich and too poor! You turn the station on her radio, and there's no saying what you'll get. So she stormed down to the water and just stood there looking out at the waves—for an eternity. It was crazy. I mean, like, forty minutes later, she was still down there. Over a song!"

"But you think she was upset about this breakup?"

Cecilly drummed the tabletop like she was thinking about that. "Mark Stern is no great loss, believe me. He's really shown his true colors this year. He'll never stop being in high school. All he did this whole winter was hang around here, hang out with us. He never talked about where he ought to go to school or what he ought to be doing. He's turning into a giant afterbirth. *I* think . . . she was upset because *he* broke up with *her,* rather than *her* breaking up with *him.* It was a huge ego blow—first time that ever happened."

My eyes wandered to Drew. I couldn't pinpoint why, exactly, Cecilly's words didn't sit right. Last year I might have heard something like that and thought nothing of it. Now I had one foot out of high school, and it struck me that it *didn't* make sense.

"Do people really spiral to the point that she's describing, just because they don't beat their boyfriend to the punch line?" I muttered.

"Mmm. Some people do, I guess." Drew shrugged. "You and I wouldn't do that, but . . ."

I watched him, maybe understanding why he couldn't quite manage to finish the sentence. Some of you wants to reason, "Stacy's turning into a conceited ho, just like her mom." Some other part is hearing with some sort of new ears or something. And you're saying to yourself, "Wait. She stands at the water's edge, spiraling for forty minutes, because she couldn't beat Mark Stern to the punch line. Does the word *shallow* mean anything to anyone?"

"Duh, maybe she already suspected she was pregnant," I tried, but Cecilly started talking again.

"It gets worse. I don't know if you could write all her behavior off to raging pregnancy hormones. Have you seen Mrs. Kearney lately?"

Lutz looked down. "Come to think of it, I haven't."

"Just . . . go to their house. Go there and knock on the door. Get her to come downstairs. You'll die."

"Is she . . . not well?"

" 'Not *well*'? Her eyes are swollen shut. She's got twenty-five scratch marks on her face. Stacy's mom is saying Stacy did that to her. Tried to scratch her eyes out."

Lutz wrote all this down slowly.

"I mean, we all get pissed at our mothers, but is that any reason to scratch your mother's eyes out? That is so . . . *out there.*"

As Lutz wrote on, I remembered how Stacy always had this love/hate thing going with her mother. When she was with just a few of us she knew really well, she would mutter that her mom was a sleaze and lay pained hints about her golf-pros-on-the-side. But once, Todd Barnes heard that song, "Stacy's Mom," on the radio and changed the words a little to how Mrs. Kearney had it *so* going on. I thought Stacy would have laughed after the things she'd told us, but she stormed off. It was hard to feel sorry for her, even when her eyes were filling up, because she spewed as much venom toward Todd at the same time. Stacy was hard to figure. I remembered Stern used to call her "high maintenance."

"I'll look into Mrs. Kearney's injuries. Thanks. Maybe it was somebody else," Lutz muttered uncomfortably. "I think we've all heard our share of Mrs. Kearney's, um . . ." He stopped.

"What, *extramarital escapades*? What a turbo slut. I'm sorry." Cecilly laughed nervously. "I'm not here to pass judgment on anybody. But she married an absolute pig. I don't know why their family came back here. But some of my mom's friends say Mrs. Kearney got tired of living poor, and maybe after twenty-five years, her parents said, 'Fine, live with us rather than starve.' God knows they've got the room."

Lutz shrugged. He'd heard this whole schmear twenty times over. "Truthfully, I've never heard the DeWinters utter a bad word about their daughter or her husband. And I do know they sent money over the years in spite of their heartache over the marriage. Some say that Wally Kearney would send it all back."

"Still, you've heard the one about how he used to eat like a pig at the table, just to disgust Mr. and Mrs. DeWinter," Cecilly said.

Again Lutz said, "I live here."

"God, your wife's family bails you out of financial trouble, and to repay them you chronically lay farts at their dining room table to get your sons to laugh at you. Mrs. Kearney made her bed. If you're going to marry the guy who cuts your father's grass, and he turns into a slug who likes to scratch, guzzle twenty cans of beer a day, never get a real job, and turn out two sons just like him . . . that's your cross to bear, my mom says. Or put it this way: You can divorce him. But you can't go around while you're still married, just dive-bombing on any golf pro, tennis pro, plumber, electrician, or mail carrier who will have you."

Cecilly was really ripping on about the Kearneys/DeWinters, but I reminded myself that she was behind closed doors. I had never heard her like this. I mentioned it to Drew.

"You haven't been around this summer as much in the early parts of the night," he reminded me. That's when I've been writing on my blog. "It's gotten *almost* this bad."

I guessed I'd heard most of this before—just never in one gigantic serving. I also knew that Stacy's grandmother on her dad's side had been a waitress at some diner in Connecticut, and Stacy still went to visit her maybe three weekends a year. We never heard her mention her Kearney grandfather. We assumed he was either dead or long divorced.

There had also been some talk about Stacy's older brothers, but they were a lot older, like the youngest being around twenty-three. So we only knew they both turned out sludgy like the father, and the DeWinter grandparents were sick about it.

I don't think the brothers had ever been in trouble with the law, but when they moved here, they got their own place and never lived in the DeWinter house, so we weren't around them much at all. The older one supposedly always had worked with his dad on the lawn service and wanted to keep the family business going. Some hell of a family business, but that was the story flying around. The younger one always wanted to live by the ocean and saw this as his chance. He was a clammer.

The couple of times they'd been at the house picking up their father, Stacy had always seemed embarrassed by them, and she would drag us up to her bedroom and close the door. They looked kind of scary—in that scratching, swaggering, muscle-bound, "Ey! Yo!" way.

"Do you know where Mr. Kearney is living now?" Cecilly leaned forward again.

"Yes. I know." The captain wrote some more, and I jerked to face Drew again.

He laughed nervously. "Try . . . the Ocean View. Moved in with his sons."

I shuddered. I might have guessed Stacy's brothers lived down there. The name, the Ocean View, is deceiving. There is no ocean view; it's close to the clam hole, a part of the back bay that smells of dead clams at low tide, and is a series of maybe thirty one- and two-bedroom apartments. The place is used by the welfare department to house displaced families. Alas, Mystic's too-poor.

Cecilly added, "If I lived with a mother that selfish and a father who probably beat everyone while on his beer benders, I might be ready for the nuthouse, too. But I would *not* have tried to scratch my mother's eyes out. And about the gun? The last week of school, some of us were down at the McDonald's one night. Mark was there, and he told us, 'Stacy bought a gun off the Internet. It came today.' I was all, '*Why?*'

"But no one could get a straight answer out of either one of them. He kept saying, 'It's to protect herself from you bitches.' Stacy kept saying, 'I just want to be a rootin'-tootin' cowboy!' I mean, the whole concept was so sick. I never asked questions. I never thought about it again until I had the thing in my hand on the pier."

"And where were you on the pier when you heard the shot?"

"I had just about decided to go talk to Alisa. She was still standing by the rail, right where she had been talking to Stacy and Mark, but now she was all alone. She looked pissed about something."

"And what was she mad about?"

"I figured it was because Todd was still sitting there talking to True. I was going to tell her True wouldn't hone in on Todd ever, but especially not three days after their huge breakup. But I never got that far. Casey was standing between me and her."

"Did you say anything to her?"

"Yeah! Being that Mark Stern was no longer in sight anywhere, I got into it with her that she needed to ditch him, and I didn't care if she had to go out with Billy Nast to do it. Nothing against Billy, you know . . ." she stammered. "You just say things like that . . ."

The truth is, Cecilly could say things just as evilly as Stacy could. I didn't know what to make of this rootin'-tootin' talk, this scratching of one's mom's eyes. I just was vaguely suspicious there was a problem in the telling here.

"Get to the point," Drew muttered, irritated.

"So the gun went off," Lutz encouraged her.

"It sounded like a little splat in the dark, like a little fire-cracker. Casey had been spewing back in my face about how everyone needed to leave her alone about Mark. And she stopped, like, midsentence. I thought she stopped because, like me, she wanted to look closer to see what the spark was. But she reached really quick for her neck."

"Her neck? Do you mean her throat?"

"No. It was more to the side. Her neck." Her own hand flew to her neck down under her ear.

"And you think she was hit?"

"I *know* she was. I saw blood. I mean, it was dark on that pier, but it was blood. It was like black liquid rushing through her fingers."

"You saw blood rush through her fingers."

"Yes. Then she screamed."

Lutz stared at the paper for a moment, wiping his hands on his pants legs. My mind went crazy. I hadn't heard Casey scream. But I'd thought I'd heard her laugh. *Had it been a scream? Had I heard it wrong?* Finally Lutz picked up the pen again and quit staring.

"She, like, staggered backward, back where the rail had burned through, and she turned and went over the back of the pier."

"She went over frontward?" Lutz asked, and I could see where he was going. Lutz was asking, *Did she fall or dive?*

I wanted to add, *What do you mean, "she turned"? You say you couldn't see in the dark . . . Are you sure this supposed blood wasn't a shadow?* I looked at my watch again. 12:37. Endless night.

"And you say you didn't see where the shot came from?"

"No. I was watching Casey. I was afraid she was going to go over even before she went over, but there was nothing I could do. So I never thought to look until she was gone. I never saw the gun. I don't know where it went or anything.

But I do know that suddenly Stacy Kearney was standing there beside me, screaming herself."

"And where was Mark Stern all this time?"

"In the toilet. That's what True says. She saw him go in there—"

"The toilet?" The captain raised his eyebrows, and she smirked with her head down.

"Okay, so we all know there's no functioning toilet on the pier. But there's that little remaining shell of the old ticket booth. If there's too many girls around and a guy doesn't want to take a leak over the side, they'll still go in there. It's shaped just like an outhouse. It totally stinks—"

"Fine, fine." Lutz jotted down something.

She leaned forward and flopped back, as if she was getting stiff from sitting. "Here's what I think. Stacy's been going a little crazy. Maybe her drunken father beat her once too often, who knows? I think maybe she got a gun to protect herself, in case he came back to the house on some bender one night and tried to beat her mom or the DeWinters to death. As for her being pregnant, she has told me a thousand times she would never sleep with anybody in high school. She said she could never stand to risk having an abortion. But Stern is such a polecat, and obviously he got her to cave in. When he breaks up with her, she's . . . not okay, but she's making it, until she finds out she's pregnant. She wants him back, maybe wants a father for this baby, because she doesn't want to go through with an abortion like she always said she was afraid of. But he's not coming back. Because of Casey Carmody. So . . . you tell me the rest."

Lutz cleared his throat, watching Cecilly glance around again at the walls. Somehow I knew she was trying to spot a recorder.

"You don't have any idea where Stacy was coming from?" he finally asked.

She shook her head woefully. "The moon was tricky. Out and in and out . . . I could barely see Casey fall. Stacy just . . . materialized beside me. Look, I know it sounds like a total soap opera." She held up her hands defensively. "But just take away the gun for a minute. Take away the gun, and you've got the same normal high school, same normal small-town crap that goes on anywhere. I've been feeling like a freak all night because I touched a gun, but everyone did. It was just so normal the way it happened. I'm *not* a freak. We're not freaks. Okay?"

 **4**

"**T**ell True to come in here," Lutz said to Cecilly, "and you can either wait for her outside or go along home."

"I'll wait," Cecilly said. I figured Cecilly wouldn't be happy until she'd heard every last version of what happened up there.

There was a commotion by the door. Cecilly was trying to hold it closed, but fingers were coming around trying to push it open.

"Captain Lutz!" Cecilly couldn't close the door all the way because of the fingers. "It's, um . . . you know."

"Captain Lutz! I must have a word with you!"

The foreign accent that made her "with you" sound like "weese you." Drew must have recognized the voice. He laid all his weight on me to get me to move.

"Oh god. You definitely don't want to be here anymore, bro—"

I stood my ground as a face I knew peered over the officer's shoulder.

"Maybe Crazy Addy saw something and won't be talking crazy for once," I proposed.

"Ms. Gearta, please go home! I will call you, I don't have time right now—" Lutz's impatience rang through.

I stood hypnotized as Crazy Addy, aka Adeleena Gearta, managed to squeeze herself past Cecilly and go in. Her ice green eyes kind of glowed neon. Crazy Addy is in her thirties now and is a haint around these islands—someone whose voodoo store you go visit with a group of blasted friends when you want to know if your girlfriend is cheating or where you'll get accepted to college. Crazy Addy tossed crystals and then "looked in them," or she stirred up some birdbath-looking thing and said she saw things in it. We thought she was very cheesy, though the girls liked getting their future romances predicted.

At a serious time like this, Crazy Addy was as welcome as having a tooth drilled. After Eddie Van Doren's suicide four years ago, the fact that she had predicted it had permeated the island like the stink of clams. Crazy Addy felt her prediction about Eddie Van Doren's suicide should have given her word more respect with the police, though it got her nothing. The cops rarely if ever followed up on her "visions," though she came to them every couple months or so, predicting some crime. Drew's dad had a lot of fun names for her: Chinese Water Torture, Crazy Migraine, etc.

Well, here she was, waving her arms.

"Captain, I have foreseen a death. Early this morning, it will come to pass if you don't listen to me. I can feel this girl's anguish! I have seen her injuries. But the police are looking for her in the wrong place. She is not in the water!"

"Adeleena, she fell in the water, so we're looking in the water. Of course, we're hoping she made it to land, that she's fine, and doesn't realize—"

"She is not fine! And she is not in the water! There is no blood, but her injuries are intense."

"Kurt, come away from there." Drew pulled at my arm.

"I want to hear."

"All right, Adeleena." Lutz rolled his shoulders uncomfortably. "If you know so much, where is she?"

"She moves. From place to place."

"From where to where? And why? If you ever want some credibility around here, give us something—sometime—that we can use!"

"She is in anguish. She doesn't know what she's doing."

"Where?" he asked again.

"There was sand under her feet, but now there is none. I saw her feet in the crystals!"

He threw his pen down in annoyance. "The island's a pretty big place. And last time you came in here, weren't you ranting that there would be a robbery if we didn't—"

"I can't tell you why the robbers didn't rob! They changed their minds!"

"For pete's sake." He scratched his forehead, and I felt sorry for him. "Look. I've got a dozen potential witnesses to—"

"I am not leaving until you listen to me. You won't listen? A girl dies!"

He stood up. "If I hear you tell one kid on this island that you know the Carmody girl is alive and suffering, I will have you locked up for . . . disturbing the peace!"

"I cannot help what I see," she said. Her face was stirred up in some kind of anguish I didn't want to understand because I was creeped out enough. She added, "I cannot help what I am. You can thank the good Lord you are *you*. You are *safe*."

After the door slammed shut behind her, Drew muttered, "Safe from what?"

The word *safe* echoed inside my head, maybe because I wrote a whole blog last week called "Unsafe." And I hadn't known what I had meant. I'd just kept writing. ". . . feels *unsafe* to walk around a corner on this island. I feel like something's going to jump out at me. I feel *unsafe* when I look somebody in the eye, like they're going to pass some wacky judgment. The water feels *unsafe*, like it's crawling with sharks, or the back bay is crawling with toads . . ." It was definitely a weird post, but I got some cool responses from people who felt irrationally unsafe near everything from ponds and bogs to the bathrooms in school.

I decided to chase after her, but suddenly Drew was holding me instead of pushing me.

"If she says Casey's alive, I want to find out more!"

"You're asking for trouble." But he trotted along beside me back up the hallway and out the front door. I broke into a mad dash for the back of the building. I heard tires screech and saw the taillights as Crazy Addy's green van took off up the street.

I cursed, gripping my head, looking for sense.

"Let's just go back inside and wait for some news," Drew said. "You are *not* going down on that beach. And you are *not* going to chase after Crazy Addy."

I looked over and saw the lights from the beach and figured from the size of the glow, they must have a dozen spots on the water. I could hear a chopper in the distance but couldn't see it. I wondered how the hell far out at sea they were searching. It didn't sound good . . . "What did she say? Something about the officers were looking in the wrong place?"

Drew answered quietly, "Yes. And, um, nobody's dead yet, but that will change near morning. I don't suppose after you heard that much, you'll be satisfied until we go have a look in the back bay . . ."

We started toward the yacht club, which is where almost everyone we knew docks their boats.

5

"*Casey!*" A lone guy's voice floated over the water as we came around the side of the yacht club main building.

Lines of boats rested quietly dockside of four floating docks. The water was mirrorlike. The storm at sea had moved farther east, toward England, or broken up south of Greenland. The wind surely had died, which meant the ocean water was next—if it hadn't calmed already. The guy's voice was clear in the silence, and the boats were un-moving, save one thirty-footer at the end. Its mast was gently bobbing.

Drew and I ran down there to find Todd Barnes getting off the Sterns' thirty-foot sailboat. He reached a hand out. *Stern.*

"Just us," Todd said, gesturing with disappointment at the bow, implying Casey was not inside.

"Guess we weren't the only ones with ideas to look back here." Drew shuddered. "You guys didn't get your idea to search back here from Crazy Addy, did you?"

"Hell no." Stern turned his chin to the masts for the sign of another one moving. "What's that warthog up to now? Don't tell me she's got something to say about all this."

I just screamed, "*Casey!*" up to the half moon. "*You are so not funny!*"

The silence that followed made me drop my face as I fought off the sudden feeling of spiraling. Three sets of bare feet moved around in awkwardness. Stern called out next.

After he got no response he said, "We came back here just a few minutes ago. Because of the sweatshirt."

I'd been afraid I might punch him out if I so much as glanced, but I looked full at him. His eyes had some hopeful glow. "They found her sweatshirt in the water."

I stepped closer. "*My* sweatshirt? White? Huge? Says *Naval Academy* on it?"

"Yeah. It washed up."

Before I could interpret that, Barnes took hold of my shoulder. "Yeah. And it was in one piece and guess what else? Just with their flashlights, the coast guard couldn't see any traces of blood on it."

"Well . . . someone said she got shot in the neck," I forced myself to admit.

Todd shook his head like it didn't matter. "And the sweatshirt wasn't all twisted up, like she might have drowned trying to get out of it. It looked like she just . . . slipped out of it. Hopefully."

Drew read my mind. "So if she didn't get hit by a bullet, what made her fall into the water?"

"Well, here's the confusing part," Barnes said. "There was this little hole. Right about here." He pointed at his left shoulder.

I fought off panic by searching my head for what that could have meant. A hole but no blood. "Maybe it, like . . . just grazed her—like, scared her," I said. "Maybe she stumbled backward and just . . . lost her footing. She's been diving the tower at the pool since seventh grade. She's long been bragging about trying a dive off that pier, though I can't believe she'd do it . . . especially when the water was so choppy and fierce. Still . . . as long as she wasn't injured badly, I think she could have caught herself in time to cut the water, rather than slam it."

The three of them nodded in agreement, and I hoped it wasn't just to be polite.

"Maybe the hole is a barnacle bite." Drew shrugged. Barnacles are a type of shellfish, and their shells attach in multilayers to pilings. In places like the pier, which has been around for a couple generations, the razor-sharp barnacle shells are three layers deep. If Casey had been thrown against barnacles by the surf, there would have been blood on my sweatshirt.

The silence that followed was cut by Stern. "So then . . . where is she?"

Barnes shook his head. "One theory on the beach was that a riptide sucked her out, and she was too tired to swim back very quickly. Coast guard was looking for the down-sea, but it's hard to find in the dark."

The down-sea is an area usually about a mile and a half out in the water, where the riptides from the piers and jetties finally calm. They shift with the weather and the water's mood. The only way to tell where the down-seas are is to look for the start of swells toward shore and strange debris you wouldn't expect to see a mile and a half out—a surfboard, a flip-flop, a kayak oar. Funny tales have been told of things found in the down-sea by boaters, especially if the riptides are bad—everything from beach umbrellas to dog dishes. You just can't imagine how some of this stuff could find its way to the water's edge to get sucked out there.

"If there had been any blood on your sweatshirt, Kurt, it was so little that it washed clean off before the forty minutes it took to catch a wave and roll in to shore," Barnes said. "They found it under the pier, which probably implies that she got out of it pretty close to shore. There's a northern undertow tonight. If she got out of it at the end of the pier, it probably would have washed up a couple blocks north."

"So she *is* alive," Drew said under his breath, and nudged me. "Down-seas, my ass. We're gonna string her up by her toes when we catch her."

I heaved a sigh, though not enough made sense yet. It looked like Casey was alive. But she was still missing, and someone had fired a gun at her, and I was tired of having no answers.

"You should have heard, um, people . . . swearing up and down that blood ran through her fingers and out her neck," I said, trying to ignore Drew knocking me in the ankle. He was probably nervous his dad could get in some trouble if word got out that we had been listening outside the questioning room. "Can seawater wash blood out of a sweatshirt?"

"Dunno," Todd said.

"Definitely not," Stern said. "It would definitely have been a little bit pink. I *think* . . ."

Drew shook his head in disgust. "Jeezus, we're all life-guards. You would think at least one of us would know if salt water could wash blood out of a sweatshirt. They'll analyze it if she doesn't show up soon."

"For now all I can tell you is that the only blotches on it were seaweed. It had picked up some chunks under the pier. Your *Naval Academy* lettering looked pretty damn scary, like haunted-house lettering. But it was not bloody, dude."

I thought of how appropriate that was, considering my sudden qualms about the place. The thought dissolved quickly as I watched the still masts of the fifty or more sail-boats docked at the club. Not a single one moved. I couldn't decide whether to ask questions or leave things be. God knows I didn't need to end up in a shoving match with Stern. He ended the silence.

"Stacy's nuts, man, buying a gun."

So much for my self-control. "So what were *you* doing passing it around, numb nuts!"

He stepped back as I stepped up to him. "Easy, Kurt. I did *not* accidentally pull the trigger, if you've got that idea in your head."

"So who did?" I exploded again.

Drew gripped my arm, blathering that she obviously wasn't at the club and we ought to leave. I'm sure he sensed what could come down, though I shook him off.

"Who brought the damn thing to the pier?" I asked.

"I did!" Stern blasted, but then lowered both his voice and his head. "But that doesn't mean I wanted to see it go off! I was over at Stacy's house earlier tonight, making small talk with the grandparents. Stacy's so rude to them these days, it's messed up. If I didn't stick my head in the door and sweet-talk them sometimes, I think they'd die of verbal abuse. It just . . . happened. We were fooling around with it . . . you know how these things are! She shouldn't have bought it in the first place."

His explanations irritated the hell out of me. He lived about six doors down from the DeWinters, but somehow I didn't quite picture him as having the best interests of old people in his heart. I just glared.

"I wasn't looking when it went off, man!" He held his arms out. "I had just walked away from Alisa after Stacy left us. I was gonna leave, being that I can only take so many hours of her right now. I was taking a leak in the ticket booth first and just wasn't looking."

Barnes shook his head. "I didn't see it either, Kurt. Sorry."

I just looked back at Stern. The skin on his face was jumping all over the place.

"You look guilty," I muttered.

"I . . . *feel* guilty!" Mark stammered. "Casey was . . . my girlfriend!"

"What do you mean *was*?"

I shoved him hard, and suddenly Todd and Drew were in between us, in the echoes of "Take it easy . . ." and "Not the time or place, man . . ." It was just the type of slip of the tongue you'd see cops jump on during episodes of *CSI*. If somebody describes a missing girlfriend in the past tense— he tried to kill her.

Stern mewled, "I didn't mean it like that! I mean, she'll probably not want to go out with me anymore after I was passing that gun around and she took a hit! That's all!"

I watched him squirm until I couldn't stand it. "We just found out that Stacy's pregnant."

He nodded hard, like this was something he knew, though the words didn't follow quickly. "Right! So . . . why would I shoot Casey? How does A relate to B?"

I couldn't quite answer that, but I wasn't ready to leave it alone, either. "Stacy was in the ticket booth with you and . . . put you up to it . . ." I stammered one thought.

"Stacy drives a brand-new Audi, lives in a big-ass house with its own pool and tennis court! She would not be caught dead in our smelly ol' ticket booth," he said. "She'd explode first."

"You were the last known person to have the gun," I argued.

"I was not! One of Casey's friends had it, and the last I saw of it, the thing was being passed down the line. The moon went under when I had to take a leak. I have no idea where it is!"

I kept watching him as he went on adamantly, "Besides. I might feel sorry for the old people she lives with, but I don't feel sorry for Stacy. Her mood swings could draw in the tide. Breaking up with her was the best thing I've ever done! If you think Stacy had it in for your sister, why throw me into the equation? Why don't you find Stacy and see if *she* pulled the trigger?"

I didn't feel like looking for Stacy as well as my sister. I didn't feel like asking him what he was doing at Stacy's if he was going out with my sister. I was sure I'd get a runaround answer, so there was no point. "You don't sound very upset about being a father," I pointed out.

Even in light of the dull moon, I could not miss the rise in his eyebrows. "Uh . . . the kid is not mine."

Typical.

"Don't laugh, man! I'm telling you the truth!" He inched closer to me. "There is no way that kid could be mine!"

I felt Drew watching him beside me, felt Drew almost

smiling, same as I almost smiled. There's some sense of weird power in getting a polecat like Stern to say in front of three guys that he hadn't worked any magic on a girl. I didn't know if I believed him—I just wanted to watch him squirm.

"So how do you *know* it's not yours?"

"Look. We all know how her mother is. Stacy's been taking lessons, obviously."

"So Stacy cheated on you," I singsonged. "With who?"

"Hey, the boyfriend is always the last to know! But if I had ever *done it* with her, I would surely know *that*, wouldn't I?"

Ahhh, gratification. A snort slid out of Drew's nostrils. But Stern's injured prowess must have been slightly less important than saving his neck, because he went on.

"And no, we didn't 'almost' do it. Stacy always told me she was terrified of a pregnancy, good Catholic that she claimed to be. If she's so devout, couldn't the church clean up her wicked mouth? She's just afraid of being known as a side dish like her old lady, that's what. If she's really knocked up, it's somebody else's. Believe me," he stammered, "I tried. I wanted to. She kept saying no."

I wondered why I hadn't put my foot down with Casey and said, "Anybody but him, you moron." Even if Stern didn't pull the trigger, he had been trying this mutt routine on my little sister and had been a big part of the gun flying around. If it wasn't for him, probably none of this would have happened.

"So . . . she was saying no to you, but yes to somebody else." I just couldn't help grinding him down to size.

He just kept shaking his head and wouldn't look at me. "It's probably some guy from another island. She's probably hot to trot just like her mom. She's probably got some Joe down in Ship Bottom or Sea Isle. Maybe a bunch of Joes. She's seventeen-going-on-twenty-five, with a new Audi and a fake ID that looks so pristine, she could get into any fancy club she wanted to. And you know, for about the last month that we went out, I didn't know where she was half the nights."

The comment was interesting enough that I wanted to hear what he meant.

"I used to call her on her cell phone. She would tell me she was in the supermarket getting stuff for her mom, but I could hear all these voices in the background, and music, like a party. Guys' voices and stuff."

Drew and I said nothing. Stern continued, "And one time she told me she was at home, and clearly, I could hear her brothers yelling at each other in the background. They don't even speak to Stacy's mom or her grandparents anymore, let alone go in that house. I knew she was lying to me, so I made up some excuse, said, 'I'll call you right back on the house phone.' She was like, 'No! Don't call on the house phone!' She knew she wasn't at her mom's. So I don't know why she's such a big liar, but she is. There you have it."

I didn't know what we had. Being that Stacy's father was staying at the Ocean View—and being that her father was a general embarrassment to her mom's family—maybe she was embarrassed to say that she got a twitch one night to go see her father and brothers. It made sense in a way.

My mind was bobbing all over the place, so Drew asked the important question. "Why did Stacy buy that gun?"

"Got me." Stern spread his arms again. "She got it the last week before I broke up with her. She showed it to me and said, 'Look at this little thing! Isn't it cute?' It was wrapped in a handkerchief, and when she unfolded the handkerchief, my eyeballs almost flew out of my head. I held it. I couldn't help it. But I didn't ask anything, like where she got it, or how, or how come."

"Why not?" Drew asked in irritation.

Stern squirmed again. "I guess because . . . I knew I wouldn't get a straight answer. When did you ever get a straight answer out of Stacy?"

I felt that for once Stern had nailed down a truth. Maybe that was why Stacy could make you so jumpy. She could laugh and joke and threaten and entertain thoroughly in a crowd. But she never *talked* about anything. She never said how she *felt* about anything. That's when a friend really becomes a friend—when they talk to you about something important to either you or them. Stacy acted like she didn't have problems, or when she did, they surely were not worth discussing. It was all chatter with her—sometimes fun, sometimes mean and hard to take, but rarely serious.

"I mean . . . I was the boyfriend. I was closer to her than

anybody, save Alisa. *Maybe.* If there's anything in there"—
he knocked on his head—"besides icicles and nails, I never
saw it."

But he was overstating his case.

"There's something else 'in there.'" I burst past them
and walked down to the end of the dock, staring into the
condo lights on the far side of the cove, watching the masts
of the boats docked there, despite the fact they all belonged
to summer people we didn't know.

"What, you're gonna defend her *now*?" Stern laughed
uneasily into my back as they shuffled up beside me. I almost turned and slugged him. I didn't remember seeing
Stacy with that gun at all on the pier, but I'd seen him with
it plenty. I wanted to kick her for buying the stupid thing,
but kill him for passing it around with so much mouth.

"Remember when Casey broke her neck and had to
start high school in a halo?" I asked instead.

Nobody answered, which smacked of "If you can't say
something nice about a guy's sister, don't say anything."

"I thought even my mom would go hoarse lecturing her
on being vain and insecure, and how she ought to count her
blessings she wasn't starting high school in a wheelchair instead. None of it did much good. Casey was so impossible
that I would leave the living room as soon as she came in.
Her girlfriends quit calling. Stacy wasn't too friendly with
her at that point, because Casey hadn't gone to high school
yet. But she was there, like, so many nights. And the morn-

ing before school started, she fixed up Casey's hair somehow and fixed her up with makeup . . ."

Everyone stayed quiet. I had never bothered thanking
Stacy. Some things are just between girls. But coming for
Casey on the first day of school must have had all the appeal
of crawling through a briar patch. I heard a laugh and realized it was mine. "I mean . . . most of the time, Stacy was
doing her Stacy routine. You know—'Casey, shut the fuck
up before I shove this mascara tube up your nostril . . . ,'
'Listening to you whine is as fun as drinking dish soap—get
over yourself before I puke on your shoe . . .' La-la-la."

"See? She's a troll!" Stern said, and I wondered if he
brought a new depth to the meaning of *idiot.*

Drew mumbled down at our feet, "Proverbs twenty-six
four," which is this very cool saying that we both like:
"Don't answer a fool in his folly, lest you become like him."

I let Stern rant on a little. "You want some motive, Carmody? Maybe I've got some. I'm not saying for sure, but
tonight when I was at her house? Stacy asked me to go back
with her."

I turned as slowly as possible, considering this was news
to me.

Mark shrugged. "I said no . . . I was with Casey now."

"Did she get mad?" Drew asked.

"Yeah. I mean . . . no. I mean, she's, like, the mystery
bitch. Hard to read. She started laughing in that evil way of
hers, and right in the middle of it, she started crying. So she

was, like, laughing and crying. And then she says to me, 'Forget I ever asked that. I don't know what comes over me sometimes . . . ,' as if she suddenly 'remembered' she was too good for me. She was *always* acting too good. Even when we went out. It got on my nerves totally. I stuck around, thinking I would finally get a piece, but I didn't even get that."

"All right, let's just go." Drew jerked on my arm before giving me time to contemplate a new definition for the term "fucking pig." Stern didn't seem to realize I'd apply his little philosophies to my own sister. "Let's leave conversations like this to the cops! They'll analyze the sweatshirt for evidence. They'll order a paternity test!"

Drew kind of spit all that over his shoulder as he pulled me along, and I heard Stern say, "Go ahead! They can order anything they want . . . ," then I was glad to be out of earshot of his donkey voice.

"Let's go to the beach," I muttered to Drew.

"As soon as a cop sees you, they'll have someone drive you right back down to the station. In fact, they're going to notice you're missing any second and send a car out to—" Drew stopped dead at the same time I did, seeing someone in a hooded white sweatshirt, sitting on the front steps of the yacht club. The place was closed and dark, but the white sweatshirt almost glowed. I forgot for a moment that they had found my sweatshirt, and I tore over going, "Casey?"

I was within five feet when I heard "Not Casey," coming from the girl. Her hood was up. She pulled on her earlobe and said, "Sounds like . . ."

Charades. Casey sounds like . . . I remembered, disappointed and annoyed, that Stacy had been wearing a white hooded sweatshirt tonight, also.

"What are you doing here?" I asked.

After a moment she stood up, not pulling the hood down. "Same thing you are."

Her face caught the glow of the moonlight. If anyone found Stacy Kearney beautiful, it was probably due to the fact that she was tall and thin and had nice blond streaks in her hair. There was nothing much to notice about her face. She had a thin line of a mouth that widened into a smile for her ornery moments, but her eyes never laughed. You'd be hard-pressed to say what color they were. But now there was some strange softness behind their hardness.

I guess it would be accurate to say that Stacy looked like she'd been slapped in the face five times and still refused to cry. Her throat got in some sort of swallowing spasm, and I just waited, frozen, because she looked so strange.

But when she snapped out of it, her voice was surprisingly even. "Okay, I checked every boat on every dock here before Mark-the-Shark showed up. I looked inside the cabins even if they were locked. The only other boats Casey would probably be on are docked at the Moorings. Alisa's down there. Or was. It's closer to the beach than this, so maybe she went home, but you can catch her on her cell phone."

She looked me square in the eye and must not have liked what she saw. She stammered only slightly. "Y-you know the number."

"Stacy's had it bad for Kurt Carmody for a while . . ."
Cecilly's words banged through my head, if for no better
reason than they were easier to think about than whether
Stacy was pretending to be an innocent searcher. If Stacy
felt anything for me right now, even sorrow, you just would
never know. I might as well be a boss at a job she doesn't
like or hate. But she refused to break this stare-off, and it
left me slightly less apt to think she was guilty of much,
though her attitude seemed challenging and, under the circumstances, pretty tasteless.

"Stacy, why in the hell did you buy a gun?" I asked, surprised at the softness of my tone.

She looked out toward the water, where Stern and Barnes
were sitting on pilings and talking in low voices. She reached
into the huge pocket of the sweatshirt and fumbled around.
I stood rooted, thinking she had the missing gun in there.
But after a moment she brought out a cigarette and a lighter.
I'd have sworn there was nothing else in the pocket.

As she flicked her lighter, my hand went to her wrist.
"Don't," I said.

As I'm not usually in people's business, that probably
tipped her off that I knew a couple things. She paused only
for a second, then lit the thing anyway. She inhaled deeply
and sent a slow exhale over the top of my head. I tore my
eyes from her challenging ones, thinking, *Great. Hurt a baby
just to be strong on me. What the hell is wrong with you?*

"Let's go, buddy," Drew murmured.

But she hadn't answered my question yet. I was entitled.

"Unless you're going to ask if I fired a gun at your sister, I don't think you have a right to ask me anything." She flicked ashes.

"Did you fire a gun at my sister?"

She took another long drag of the cigarette. "No."

I wanted to strangle her as she exhaled over my head again, but the swallowing spazzes came back over her throat and the strange look returned to her face.

"And where were you when the gun went off?" I kept it up anyway.

She kind of flinched, then laughed sadly at the ground. I could never understand tough girls like this. Stacy could buy a gun, then pull a total hurt-and-astonished routine when I imply she might have fired it. That's what her look absolutely was—blatant hurt—but before I could rub the goddamned situation in her face, she turned toward the street and dropped the cigarette in the gutter without bothering to stomp on it with her Reefs.

"Drama queen," Drew mumbled at her back. Then he said utterly loudly, "And where will you be if the cops want to ask you some stuff?"

"At home," she hollered straight up, without turning or breaking stride.

"You better be," he whispered, and it was my turn to haul him along, back to the police station, before they realized I had left and decided *I* somehow looked suspicious.

6

The commotion inside the police station had got well under way, as kids overflowed from Captain Lutz's office out into the front corridor. Obviously the cops had been rounding them up. I could see one other cop in Lutz's office now, a young cop they called Little Jack, even though "Big" Jack had been retired since I was nine. My parents lugged Casey and me to Big Jack's retirement dinner, where it became known to me that Sergeant Jack Cantrell had personally piggybacked seventy-some people from their flooded houses to higher ground in the March storm of 1963. Some cops' names shouldn't be used over again.

My eyes scanned hopefully for Casey. I didn't see her. But my eyes locked with True's, and if Casey had been found she would have rushed me. She was just standing off to the side with Cecilly. True was wearing a dark sweatshirt, her arms crossed, and she didn't exactly look happy.

I headed for them, passing two of Casey's friends who were sniffing up scared tears. I just pretended I didn't see the girls. I didn't need anyone crying in my face yet, and True and Cecilly looked only a little tired and irritated.

"You talk to Lutz?" I asked.

True shook her head. "I started to. About a minute into it two officers brought in the sweatshirt. They took some pictures, and now it's on its way to some lab. I saw it, though. There wasn't any blood on it. Just mud and seaweed."

I glanced at Cecilly, who looked ready to burst, and she let fly with what I already heard her tell Lutz. "I saw blood, Kurt. I still think it was blood and . . . you're entitled to know what really happened."

I wasn't surprised by Cecilly's stubbornness. Somehow everything she said was a "fact" to her.

Drew changed the subject. "We just checked the yacht club. We saw Stern and Barnes down there looking. Saw Stacy, too."

"Yeah, what was she doing?" Cecilly asked. "Pretending to be hunting?"

I said nothing.

Cecilly put her hand on my arm and looked genuinely concerned. "Not that I think Casey . . . isn't going to be found. But we know a shot got fired, and I think I know who fired it."

I wasn't supposed to know the load of stuff she'd told Lutz, so I kept up the quiet routine.

"Up on the pier I had seen Stacy talking to Alisa, so I assumed she was with Alisa when we heard the shot. But I just overheard Alisa say to Little Jack that Stacy had walked away from her, and she didn't know where she had gone. I never saw Stacy until after the gun went off. Suddenly she was beside me, screaming Casey's name along with everyone else."

Drew groaned, so I didn't have to. I could see Alisa Cox sitting beside Lutz's desk. Little Jack was sitting in Lutz's chair, watching Alisa fill out the form each of us had to fill out before giving a statement.

"She just got here," Cecilly said. "She was looking for Casey down at the Moorings with Casey's friends. One of the day-shift officers also showed up back there, and he had a flashlight. They looked in every boat. She's not there."

"So Alisa's going to talk to Captain Lutz now?" I asked.

"She's in line," True muttered. "I'm still next."

"Casey's not at our house, she's not at the yacht club, and she's not at the Moorings," I spat out, feeling more and more ready to look at the whole truth. It suddenly seemed like a more sane deal than so much confusion. I made myself acknowledge that my sister could be a mile and a half out, treading water . . . or something even worse. I looked at my watch. 1:25. At least my parents were in the air and wouldn't be calling for a few more hours.

"True!" Lutz's voice echoed from the corridor, and I

could barely see his eyes raise over the crowd of kids. True moved toward him, and they disappeared down the little corridor where Drew had found me, to go into the questioning room.

"So really . . . what did Stacy have to say for herself?" Cecilly asked.

I shrugged. "Said she didn't do it."

"Did she say what inspired her to buy a gun?"

"No."

"What is up with her and the weird, goddamned secrets?" Cecilly said to nobody in particular. She tapped one foot on the floor, glaring over my shoulder. "There's who you ought to talk to." She jerked her head, and I turned to see Alisa. "She knows a lot more than she's saying."

"About what?" I asked.

"About *everything*. The way the two of them always have their heads together, it's obnoxious. I used to think it was just a random party move. You know: Act like you've got some serious, secret business, because it makes you look important. But they do it so much, I really think Stacy confides in her. Actually tells her stuff. Because tonight Alisa's been saying Stacy couldn't have done it. She wouldn't say why not, but she's the only one saying that. So she either knows something, or *thinks* she knows something."

Alisa was standing now, nodding at Little Jack as she handed the report form back to him. She turned and locked eyes with me over the tops of a couple heads. She's not tall, but I am. Something like a polite, distracted smile formed on her face, though she looked away again fast and went to sit in a chair just outside Lutz's office to wait her turn.

"Gimme a stab at her," Cecilly said, and patted my arm before heading over there. I didn't want to follow her with Drew and make Alisa feel so put on the spot that she clammed up. But I didn't want to sit back here, either, and listen to girls sniff.

Drew followed me without even asking where we were going.

We lucked out. It seemed Lutz had totally forgotten about this little corner of his new wing. With most of the officers still on the beach, we were able to edge up to the window.

Lutz was watching True with his hands crossed over his chest. This time he looked upset. True was red and nervously picking at her fingers.

"How is it," he asked, "that the head of our church's youth group can get herself into situations like this?"

She only sighed and muttered, "I'm sorry."

"Oh, really. Why can't you . . . inspire people *not* to go on that pier instead of ending up there yourself? Isn't that what leaders do?"

She grabbed her long ponytail and gripped it in dread. "Only . . . I'm not really a leader. I do the youth group for my dad. He wants me to. And, you know . . . my big sister Melanie turned out to be such a PK. I just can't do that to him. He's not perfect, but he doesn't deserve that."

PK stands for Preacher's Kid, and PKs are often known

for being totally badly behaved, as Melanie proved over the years. She's twenty-one now and finally trying to straighten out, but when she was True's age, she'd had a string of run-ins with authorities for shoplifting, drunk driving, possession of marijuana—you name it. Now she has a baby boy that True brings to the beach sometimes to give Melanie a break.

"But it puts big-time pressure on me, because I'm just not a leader. I just . . . don't know how to say no to my dad."

"Sounds like he's not the only one you can't stand up to," Lutz said, though his tone was not harsh. She just raised and lowered her eyebrows, staring at her thumb while she picked at it. He finally noted, "You have loud, unruly friends."

True brought her wrists up to her eyes and rubbed. When she flopped them down, her eyes were glassy, starting to spill. "Yeah, and I'm sick of it. I've been sick of it for months. I'm basically here because Cecilly wanted to come, but I think she saw a lot more than I did. I just want to tell what I know, and once I leave here I'm dropping all these kids. Every one of them. I wanna be . . . I wanna be good, Captain Lutz. I just don't know how to do it with them as my friends."

She broke off for a few good sniffs, and I found myself glancing sideways at Drew. He looked as uncomfortable as I felt. I had too many worries on my plate, but the concept barreled through them and landed at the front of my brain: True was talking about *me*. She was clumping *me* in with Stacy, Alisa, Stern, Barnes . . .

And so was Lutz. *Am I loud and unruly?* I didn't feel like that.

I started to wonder about something else: how people can be so close to one another that you have a nickname for your crowd, and how you can know so little about them. I stood watching True, feeling guilty that I really had no idea what she would say to Lutz—or how she would say it—or how she would feel about it.

"The Mystic Marvels!" She finally forced herself to laugh while sniffling. "You know what I've been wondering while I was sitting out there? I've been wondering if the kids who live down at the Ocean View think they're *el-perfecto,* too. I don't know if anybody thinks of themselves as bad. We all have excuses. And we all like each other. How can someone be bad if you like them? *Huh?*"

Lutz didn't answer her. But she didn't look like she was waiting for an answer. "How can people be *bad* when they're *nice?* We're nice people! At least . . . I feel like we're okay. I really have to, um, step outside myself to say this. I have to step outside of me and pretend I'm reading about a bunch of kids in a magazine or something, kids who sneak up on a pier and get all looped, and someone brings a gun, and everyone thinks it's funny until some . . . pretty girl gets shot and goes over the side. If you switched the dilapidated old pier for an abandoned old building, do you know what? If I read that I would think, 'Wow, they're probably on the skanky side.' Seriously. I would think, *Maybe they're*

*somewhat cool, but they're also skanks, and they just can't
smell themselves anymore.* The Mystic Marvels—ha. We're
like low tide. You can't smell the low tide if you've been
breathing the island air long enough."

True scratched her forehead nervously, then raised her
head, like she was looking right at us. "I think . . . I hate my
friends."

I backed away instinctively, but Drew didn't, though he
smiled uncomfortably as I turned my back on them. "My
dad and I played around with this room right after it was
finished," he said softly. "She can't see you. She's seeing a
reflection of herself. But it sure is weird, isn't it? Hearing
what people will say when they don't know their friends are
listening?"

"Why didn't she ever tell us she felt stressed like this?" I
managed to whisper. "She trusts a cop more than us."

"Lutz is magic," he murmured back. "That's why he's
here, and everyone else is out searching. He'll take his
measly time, with her and everybody else, and he'll end up
with more goop than a tube of Crest."

I tried to fight a feeling of betrayal, what with True saying to Lutz things she'd never said to us. It seemed hypocrit-
ical to feel betrayed, being that I hadn't said anything
to her about the Naval Academy. I hadn't trusted her to understand. She trusted a cop; I trusted a blog board. And I
suddenly wondered if Billy Nast trusted his friends. And
I wondered what your relationships are based on if trust

doesn't come into it. I felt empty—empty enough to pull back from fretting about friendship and remind myself of the most important problem.

"Let's hope Lutz doesn't take forever finding out his goop." I looked at my watch. 2:01. "It's all very interesting, but excuse me, my sister's missing."

"Every other cop on the force and the entire coast guard are responsible for *finding* Casey." Drew yawned, but with sympathy. "He's responsible for finding out *what happened* to Casey. He can take weeks. But if his timing isn't gelling with your gut right now, we can go back out—" He sounded kind of pleading, and I supposed he was worried about his dad catching him back here. But he was already dead for holding the gun, and your dad can only totally kill you once.

"No." Who could pass this up?

"I want to . . . to move down to the Jesus House," True finally got out. "You know those kids who are here in the summers that rent the house up Bayberry Road, and they go to the beach and drive everyone crazy while giving out religious tracts? I wanna go with them."

Lutz cleared his throat and muttered something I couldn't hear, but it had the word *escapism* in it.

"You don't understand!" she said. "I want to be *good*! I am sick of my life!"

"What'd she ever do that was so awful?" Drew grumbled beside me.

My mom always says that my dad's study of psychology,

just to build his characters, makes him a better shrink than Cecilly's dad. He can keep me hypnotized at the dinner table for an hour, blathering on about how families act strange, just because they're families, and how family weirdness is all tied up together. I pulled instinctively from what I figured he would say. "Someone in the family has to pay for Melanie's sins."

Drew stared at me sleepily. Again he muttered the word *profound,* which made me raise my usual smirk. But maybe being "profound" all the time was why I couldn't talk to Drew about the Naval Academy. Maybe I liked the way he admired most of the stuff I said. Maybe I didn't want to sound like an idiot and have to watch his face seize up for once when I opened my mouth.

Maybe all this stuff about me holding my tongue on the island was about having a big head. Maybe I'd walk out of here tonight feeling like a conceited jerk, along with feeling irresponsible and like a horrible big brother.

Lutz was giving True some spiel about how it might be good for her to try practicing the Golden Rule before moving into the Jesus House, and seeing how that went.

"Like you could tell me everything you know now. That would be *golden.*"

She shifted around uncomfortably in her chair, threw her head back, and stared up at the ceiling. "I'll tell you anything you want! Problem is, I didn't see anything. I was sitting there with Todd Barnes, who was trying to whisper in my ear, and all I could think about was Alisa over by the rail watching. They just broke up. I thought the pistol crack came from the stars! I thought it was, like, fireworks that never burst open . . . something. I didn't see Casey fall, and I didn't see where Stacy Kearney was, before or after."

He wrote all that down but looked like he was taking his time about it, deliberating over something. He finally said, "You mention Stacy. Do you have some reason to think she was involved?"

I almost laughed at how he could take things right back to the bare beginnings and play totally innocent so well. At two in the morning.

"Yeah . . . but . . ." True's swallowing reminded me of Stacy's swallowing. True was the middle child in a very flamboyant family, almost like a pigeon in with a bunch of seagulls, despite her being pretty cute—cuter than her sister Melanie by far. Maybe she couldn't get a word in edgewise around that family and decided her thoughts didn't matter. I could tell by her bobbing jaw that this was agonizing for her.

"Golden Rule," Lutz reminded her, and though she didn't move from that ceiling-staring, sprawled-out, gangly way, she started to talk. It was low. I had to breathe silently to catch it all.

"A few nights back, Mark told Cecilly that he thought Stacy was cheating on him. He said that the last month they were going out he couldn't find her a lot of nights. Cecilly just . . . had to know. That's Cecilly's way. I'm used to her nosiness. Maybe I shouldn't be."

"Okay," Lutz said.

"The other day we were on the beach and Stacy got mad because Cecilly was dominating the radio. A lot of the girls really hate this thing about Cecilly. She doesn't exactly have good, um, *boundaries?* No matter whose radio it is on the beach, she'll just act like it's hers and turn the station whenever she doesn't like a song." True took a big breath, let it out, and then talked on to the ceiling. "Stacy was in the mood from hell anyway. She went down to the water's edge to get away from everyone, I guess. So Cecilly reaches in Stacy's bag, pulls out her cell phone, and starts to look at the phone log."

True cast her eyes down to Lutz. I recalled Cecilly talking about that day on the beach. She'd mentioned Stacy's bad mood but nothing about grabbing her cell phone. I listened closely, feeling a little betrayed.

"She wanted to see who Stacy had called . . ." Lutz encouraged True.

"Yeah. Cecilly had her beach chair facing the dunes just in case Stacy turned around, and she kept saying to me, 'Keep an eye out and tell me if she starts to come.' I don't know . . . Here's one reason I don't like the Marvels anymore. I think that is really a raunchy thing to do. I'm, like, up to my neck in raunch. Stacy's being a jerk, Mark's gossiping, Cecilly's investigating . . . and here's the worst. I was laughing. While Cecilly was looking in that phone log? I couldn't help it. I simply could not tell her to put that phone down! There's this evil witch part of me, too, that wanted to know if Stacy was cheating."

True stopped, and I wondered if Lutz felt like he ought to be wearing two hats—an investigator hat and a shrink hat. He didn't try to pull her back to the main topic or anything. I don't think he said much more than "Cecilly find any intrigue?"

"Too much! Not only did she look at the numbers. I thought that was crass enough. But she came across three numbers in a row she didn't recognize. You know . . . we all know each other's phone numbers. So she hits CALL to see who the first one was."

"To see if it was another guy?" Lutz asked.

"Yeah. But it wasn't. It was . . . a shrink."

"A what?" Lutz asked, though I suppose he'd heard as well as I had.

"A shrink. It was a psychotherapy office of some sort— the Mainland Center for Mental Health, or something like that. And Cecilly's dad is a shrink, and it wasn't her dad's office, so that set Cecilly off. She figured Stacy must have some totally wild problem up her butt if she wouldn't trust an islander."

Lutz wrote a couple of things. "So Cecilly hung up after hearing it was a doctor's office?"

"Yeah. Then she called the other two numbers she didn't recognize."

"And?"

"Both shrinks. Two more shrinks. It looked to me like Stacy was shopping around for a shrink. At that point even I was like, 'Cecilly, put the damn thing away—that is so not your business.' But who ever listens to me around here?" She let out a tired laugh. "Nobody, that's who."

"So . . . I guess we could say that Stacy felt like she needed to see a psychiatrist," Lutz said, and wrote a note.

"Yeah, I guess you could say Stacy is messed up. Especially now. I suppose you heard about the pregnancy."

Lutz nodded.

"So Stacy's pregnant and wanting to see a shrink, probably because she has to decide whether to terminate the pregnancy, and it's making her crazy. She really loves babies. She's the only one who seems really happy when I bring little Matthew to the beach to give Mel a break. But she wouldn't want to hurt her grandparents. Everybody has hurt Mr. and Mrs. DeWinter. I think Stacy wants to be the only one who doesn't."

"Sounds like a lot to cope with. A therapist could help her sort it out."

"Maybe. But maybe it's too late. That's what Cecilly says. You probably know by now it was Stacy's little gun up on the pier. She bought it last month, yada, yada, yada."

Lutz grunted, indicating he knew.

Yeah, this looked horrible for Stacy. Something stubborn inside of me just didn't want it to be her who shot at my sister. Maybe I would have barely questioned it a year ago, but now it seemed like a major leap from Stacy bought a gun and we don't know why, to Stacy brought the gun to the pier and pointed it at my sister and fired. It gave me the creeps how easily people seemed to be able to make that leap—about somebody who was supposedly their friend. It was almost like they *wanted* it to be true.

And I wondered again why Cecilly hadn't told Lutz about the phone-log search on the beach. It was either because she'd told him so much that she couldn't fit in everything, or because it was inconvenient to her to make herself look bad. She'd been on a mission to make Stacy look bad. The truth wouldn't have fit the goal.

Lutz asked, "Did Cecilly ever mention the phone log to Stacy? Confront her, maybe? Add to the girl's woes?"

"No," True said. "But she probably did worse. Cecilly's mom is this total gossip hag. I mean, Mrs. Holst can be really fun and everything, but she's got this thing about psychoanalyzing everyone on the island and doing it with her mouth open. I don't think she means anything by it, but, still. And she does this one other thing I hate, which is play tennis with Mrs. Kearney as if they're friends. I think Mrs. Holst likes to look rich, too. But then she'll go around and rag on the woman all the time. Truth? I don't think the kids on the island would know about Mrs. Kearney running around with other men if it weren't for Cecilly's mom."

I wondered about that for a moment. It's not like we've made it our life's ambition to know what grown-ups on our island are up to. I had heard about Stacy's mom from kids, not grown-ups. But Cecilly's house was a hub. It was a big roomy house on the bay, with a great family room, so we were always over there, looking at the big-screen TV and eating whatever great stuff Cecilly's mom whipped up for us.

"Anyway, Cecilly told her mom about the shrinks, knowing that her mom wouldn't be able to stand it and would say something to Mrs. Kearney. Did you hear a story tonight about Mrs. Kearney having her eyes scratched out?"

Lutz pretended, I think, to look at his notes and then said, "Yes."

"Well, I'd imagine Stacy's mom brought up to Stacy a few pretty private phone calls to shrinks, which would have outraged anybody. Not that you should scratch your mother's eyes out, but I don't want to be so quick to judge Stacy. I haven't lived with her mom and dad, and I haven't been pregnant."

"But you heard Cecilly tell her mother this? Hoping she would tell Mrs. Kearney?" Lutz asked while writing.

True stared at the ceiling so long, I felt my stomach bottoming out. She finally said, "No. I heard Cecilly *tell me* that she was going to tell her mother . . . *just because* she knew it would get back to Mrs. Kearney, and that ought to be a classic blowup."

There was a long silence that was covered by Lutz's writing and my stomach gurgling a lot.

"So . . . Cecilly told her own mother just to stir up the water." Lutz repeated this unbelievable news.

True's eyes had turned glassy again. She wiped a tear off her face. "Thank god we didn't know about the pregnancy at that point! But I already told Cecilly tonight . . . I said, 'Listen to me, for once. If you tell your mother about something like a pregnancy, just to stir up a shit storm, consider me no longer your friend.' But you know what?"

"What?" Lutz asked.

"I don't think I want her as my friend anymore, anyway. I need to find new friends. *All* new friends. I am so tired. I'm, like, so, so tired. . . ."

7

I was expecting to see Alisa come in next, but there were a bunch of kids out in the back lobby whose parents were not as close to Chief Aikerman as Alisa's were. Their parents were wanting to take them home, complaining mildly about it being the middle of the night. So those kids came in, one after another. I was in some sort of exhausted-but-hypnotic trance. I stood there for the next hour and a half, watching person after person give a five- or ten-minute statement. They'd all heard Stacy Kearney was pregnant, that the father was Mark Stern, who had been going out with Casey Carmody. They hadn't been able to see whether Casey had been hit, but everyone presumed she had been. Some saw her stumble and go over backward; some saw her stumble and turn and fall forward. Some saw blood gushing from somewhere; some saw no blood. Some heard a scream; some heard a laugh.

They'd all heard that Stacy had bought a gun and felt that was weird beyond reasoning. Because they all wanted to focus on Stacy, they ended up answering a question that was becoming a habit for Lutz: "Aside from this gun, what is it about Stacy Kearney that you don't like?" I guess, like me, he was trying to weed out truth from jealousy, truth from follow the leader.

For one junior girl the problem was how Stacy would mention her tennis lesson in school, "just to remind people that hers was the house with the tennis court." For another it was that she gunned her Audi in the school parking lot, "just so that people would turn and be reminded that she drove a more expensive car than half the teachers." When asked how they could know her motives, the answer always was, "You can just tell."

One guy in Casey's grade decided Stacy was "a tease" who would "bang on any guy so long as he was from New York or Martha's Vineyard, and not from around here." I wondered how he would know that, being that he was too young to have a chance in hell of finding out personally.

I knew that all of these complaints, though different, shared something. But at 3:30 I couldn't exactly think of what it was. Finally Alisa came in the little room, and I decided to stay, to hear what Stacy's only friend had to say in her defense. She had defenses so obvious that I couldn't believe I hadn't thought of them. And yet having not thought of them, some astonished me.

"**T**hank you for staying until this ungodly hour," Lutz muttered as Alisa came through the door. His eyes had started to look swollen and red like everyone else's.

"I'm missing my beauty rest." Alisa sat down in the chair and folded her hands with slightly too much drama. She was known as our "girlie girl" in the Mystic Marvels and was always doing stuff like putting one finger under her nose and raising her pinkie to sneeze, "*Chewwww!*"

But she had a nice wit, too—the type that could make you laugh when she kept a deadpan face. She'd just done it with the "beauty rest" remark, but before Lutz could decide whether she was serious, she went on with her toned-down sarcasm. "I can't understand what you need me for. I suppose you've heard it all. Stacy bought a gun. Stacy's a meanie. A bitch-queen, a bitch-hag, a bitch-tease, a bitch on wheels, a killer bitch, a—"

"I got it without the graphic synopsis. I'm more interested in hearing what *you* think about tonight."

Alisa went for the facts, but there weren't too many. She had started to walk to the climbing mounts to go back to the dunes so she wouldn't have to look at Todd flirt with True Blueman. She didn't see anything, didn't hear the shot, didn't hear Casey hit the water, didn't hear anything but people screaming after Casey fell. I wondered why she'd waited until after three in the morning to report only that. She could have gone home and come back after she woke up. Whatever her reasoning, Lutz took advantage of a good op. "I'll be honest with you. A lot of people are suspicious of your best friend. I thought maybe you could give me a new thesis to work with."

Alisa blinked at him a couple times in her dramatic way and said, "I know Stacy can be moody. I know she bought a gun. I know . . ." She raised her hand like a kid in class, but with her pinkie falling away. "Everyone on the island now knows about her pregnancy, and it was *I* who told. I am responsible for that. I was stupid. That's our crime, Stacy's and mine. Our only crime . . . is that *I* was stupid."

"What do you mean?" Lutz asked.

"If I hadn't told about the pregnancy, nobody would think a lot of melodramatic island twaddle about . . . Stacy needed to get rid of Casey Carmody. I've never heard of anything so out there."

"But you yourself said Stacy has personality problems." Lutz stumbled a little.

"I said *problems*—scratch the personality. I think she's . . . responding as normally as anyone would if they had her life. In fact, I think she's a saint!"

"Nothing's perfect, but most of the people who came through here tonight think her life is pretty nice."

"*Mm, mm, mm.*" Alisa giggled but barely smiled. "Her house and car are 'pretty nice.' It's what goes on *inside* the house that makes the person. But leave it to everyone on this godforsaken island to forget that so quickly. It's convenient, isn't it, if you've got a personal problem with rich people? And just about everybody does. Why is it that everyone loves to see the rich person get flushed down the toilet? Why is it people will spend four dollars to buy a magazine just so they can read about some Hollywood star's divorce? Or arrest? Or bad luck? I have no idea what Hollywood crimes have actually been told truthfully, but at least I have the brains to say I don't know." She giggled again at her little piece of irony. "What I'm blown away by is the way people act. People *want* the rich to be guilty."

"People *want* Stacy to be guilty," Lutz parroted. His eyes looked really tired.

"That's part of it. The money stuff. The rest of it?" She sighed and rubbed her eyes. "It has to do with the fact that she's . . . different."

"A number of people told me she bought a gun."

"Yeah, that's different." Alisa giggled again, some high-pitched but tired thing.

"Can you verify that?"

"Verified." She nodded with a groan. "I heard about it a while ago, in a McDonald's one night. All Stacy did was admit to having bought it. We never talked about it again."

"So you have no idea why?"

"Nope. *That's* different, too, isn't it? She'd admit to buying a thing like that and then offer no explanation. She's got a flare for drama."

"She's got no vendetta against Casey Carmody?"

"No. Don't get Stacy wrong. She's kind of riled up and wrathful in her personality. But it's just a sprinkle that kind of goes everywhere—a little. She's got no deep problems with any one person."

"So you don't feel she fired a gun up on the pier?"

"No."

"Do you know where she was when the shot was heard?"

"No. She'd left me and Mark."

"Heading in which direction?"

Alisa inhaled and thought about it for a long time before she exhaled and spoke. "It's hard to say. The moon went under. She turned her back, started straight across the pier, like to where Kurt Carmody was talking to Billy Nast. But the night, um, swallowed her. Not that I was paying total attention. My ex-boyfriend was flirting with another girl right in my face. Stacy's ex-boyfriend was spewing around that Stacy was pregnant. I was trying to live with the fact that despite my magnificent brain fart in telling her dark secret to Mark Stern, Stacy wasn't mad at me. She told me it was a brain fart, but then she was trying to console me for feeling guilty. How's that for a decent friend? I just wanted to take my IQ and go die somewhere."

"You sound very convinced she has a lot of good qualities."

"Beyond good."

"Tell me about them."

Alisa drew in a deep breath. "Stacy's generous. She'll give anyone the shirt off her back. She got a credit card from her grandfather for whatever stuff she needs. She could be blowing huge wads on herself. Her grandfather's so glad to finally have her in his life, I don't think he'd care if she charged diamonds and pearls. Last year True Blueman had this toothache and confessed to us she hadn't seen a dentist in four years because her dad doesn't have dental insurance. Well, she went to the dentist, had two teeth drilled, got the usual kid sealant she never got when she was small. It cost a lot. Guess who paid for that?"

"True didn't mention that," Lutz noted.

"True doesn't know. I walked in on Stacy one night, and she was giving Dr. Rubenstein's office her credit card number. She was saying to call the Bluemans' house and tell them it was covered by the bogeyman. Call Dr. Rubenstein and ask him whose credit card number is on True Blueman's dental bill."

Lutz made a note of that. I thought he was going to ask

a question, but Alisa was on a roll. "Then she hangs up the phone and turns around and sees me standing there. She was all, 'Bitch, did you hear that? Tell, and I'll have the Connecticut mafia come fucking waste you.' If you can get past Stacy's mouth, she's generous to a fault. And she's also Johnny-on-the-spot if you're in trouble."

"Like how?"

"I could give you hundreds of examples. Take . . . she stood by Casey when she broke her neck and no one else could stand to hear her whine about that halo a minute longer. We were all like, 'Casey. Can you be even *slightly* less superficial? Frankly, nobody gives a damn what you look like.' Stacy seemed to . . . understand. She's like a mother. Everybody's mother."

"I wouldn't say anyone tonight described her as 'a mother.'"

"You're right; they were describing her as a thoughtless b-word. Right? In her case her mother's the thoughtless b-word. Stacy's a package deal. All the caring, all the mouth."

"Even if you did spill her secrets, it sounds like you're a good friend to her," Lutz noted.

Some of the defensiveness in Alisa's face softened away. She looked downward and said with a pinch in her voice, "I know her better than anybody. But there are lots of things about Stacy that nobody knows. Not even me."

Lutz froze the pen on the page. After a long silence he said, "The guys on the force call this the questioning room.

You can still smell the paint on the walls, can't you? I'm hoping I'll get to call it the answering room. Answers to investigations come, but only after the questions are raised You can raise your questions here, too, Alisa. Maybe we can find the answers together."

I wondered if she was getting to whatever had kept her here until three in the morning. She stared at the tabletop, only sending her gaze sideways to Lutz after saying, "Okay. Here's a question: *Who's the father?*"

Lutz tapped his pen on the paper and finally said with what seemed like care, "If you're talking about the notion that Stacy is pregnant—yes, I've heard that. Do you have some reason to believe that Mark Stern isn't the father?"

"Yes. Contrary to popular opinion, not every girl sleeps with her Joe."

Mark had blathered on at the yacht club about how Stacy was no-give, I remembered hazily. And some sophomore snot had said, basically, not half an hour ago, She'll jump anything, so long as he's from the city and not from here. Even the guys she turned down called her a slut. I wondered at that.

"If you don't mind my saying so, you don't make a baby with spit." Lutz laughed uncomfortably.

Alisa stared down at her fingers, laced together so her nails were digging into the backs of her hands. "I can only say what's out there, what's been said. She told me in January she knew Mark was a horn-toad, but he was in a slump, and she figured she could cheer him up. *Little Miss Do-gooder.* There's a prime example for you. Stacy realizes a horn-toad is in a slump, so it becomes her solemn duty to become his girl-friend so she can cheer up his life. She said she could keep him under control. She told me in April she had never done it with him. She told me in June that she was so *glad* she hadn't. Last Friday I went with her to a clinic, and she turned up two months pregnant."

"Did she confess at that point to having had a lapse in judgment?"

"No."

"She didn't mention somebody else?"

"No."

"Do you . . . think she was raped? Is that why she bought a gun?" Lutz, with raised eyebrows, poised the pen to write, as if something finally made sense.

Alisa let go of a long exhale behind tightly pinched lips. I thought she might puncture the backs of her hands with her nails. "I asked when we came out of the clinic if she'd been raped, and she said no."

After a minute Lutz turned his watch slightly toward himself. "We're not so sleep deprived that you're going to pass off an immaculate conception on me. Was she propos-ing that she might have been raped and repressed the mem-ory? If that doesn't work, I'm out of . . . far-out notions."

"It's far out, but yeah, that's what she was saying. I just can't see why she would lie to me about not having any memory of being with some guy. I mean, to say something like that is a lot weirder than saying you got raped. Why add crazy to scandalous?"

"People say all sorts of nonsensical things when they've been victims of an assault. Try to explain what makes you think she really doesn't remember and wasn't just lying to you. And please don't tell me, 'Because you can just tell.'"

Alisa was probably sharper than the other girls in our crowd. We knew she pulled straight As without cracking a book, but because she never bothered mentioning it, her sharpness wasn't an issue with us. But in certain situations, it showed. She watched Lutz's eyes and, from behind them, picked up the notion that everyone before her came in making accusations about Stacy ending with "Because you can just tell."

"You know . . . if people on this island were able to 'just tell' things so easily, why was it so hard for them to see that Stacy was in obvious danger, living in her own house?"

Lutz sat frozen, but Alisa just went on. "She doesn't talk about her past much. I take it she wasn't very happy before she came here. She refuses to talk about her life in Connecticut. It's like her whole family is a taboo subject. If you mention her grandparents, she gets uptight, like her parents might be next for examination. That's been the only real, um, weirdness for me. I'm from a big family. I've got twenty-five first cousins, so I could tell stories about my family forever. It's been tough sometimes, having a friend who has nothing to say in reply—I mean *nothing, nada, zilch.* Her family, but especially her parents, are in the black hole, along with a few other subjects. Some questions you just don't bother with. If she brings up a subject herself, it's cool. If you bring it up, you'll just never get a straight answer."

So there it was: the reason Alisa had stayed until three in the morning. I just felt myself kind of float and drop as the concept of incest started coming clear. I wondered suddenly if all this eavesdropping was a good idea. I had my sister to think of, and listening in seemed more productive than sitting in the back lobby with the gossip squad. But I had never known an incest victim. A molestation victim? Probably. You hear things like that around school secondhand, and you think of it when you see the person floating around the corridors. But there's some sort of big bad leap from molestation to incest—from the guy up the street to your dad. I couldn't quite describe it any better than a leap—and it's simply not something you'd want leaping out of books and television and onto your podunk island.

I glanced at Drew, but he was just watching. We'd heard all kinds of shit tonight, and I wasn't sure he was as awake as I was.

"After the pregnancy test came back positive, twice, Stacy told me she wanted to go see a shrink, but a special kind of shrink—the kind that can hypnotize you and, after a few weeks of it, maybe pull out a repressed memory."

She looked at Lutz, and despite his being deadpan, she put her palms out as if to apologize. "I know this sounds totally crazy. But it seemed less crazy than some alternatives. Here's one thing about Stacy people don't know: She's scared of the dark. She can't walk the beach at night by herself, and in her grandparents' huge old house? She tells me she lies awake at night, like, listening for spooks. I know that old house creaks and groans all night long; I've slept there. But at this point she started talking about ghosts. Like she was having moments of wondering out loud if the ghost of Eddie Van Doren got her, or if she was carrying the spawn of Satan . . . I was all, 'O*kay*! Time for a shrink, Stacy! Good idea!'"

Lutz wrote some notes, not looking too happy. This wasn't exactly making Stacy appear sane, but I could see Alisa's dilemma—and I figured she had done right. Some things you have to try to confess to someone responsible if you care about your friend.

"So you went to a shrink?" Lutz encouraged her.

"I wish. We called a few, but they were really expensive, and Stacy only had fifty bucks cash and her credit card. She has the kind of charge that sends her grandfather an e-mail every time something's put on it. She was afraid he would see the charge and jump to the conclusion that her father had been messing with her, when that might not be true at all."

I felt Drew rise slowly to his feet beside me and decided he was now awake. We watched Lutz write, and I thought of

104

one of my dad's young girl characters swearing up and down all day that her uncle Chris was a great guy, though many nights Uncle Chris was molesting her. *The girl couldn't remember her nights during her days.* I wondered if Dad had made that up because it sounded good, but knowing how my dad loves to research human behavior, I doubted it.

Alisa apologized again. "I'm very crazed over all this myself. But I'm not going to bag on my friend when she needs me the most. God knows, none of the other people she's ever helped is going to stand by her now. Not True, not Mark, not even her family. She decided not to see a shrink because she was afraid her grandfather would leap to the wrong conclusion."

"That's quite a leap for her grandfather to make," Lutz said. "Stacy wants to see a therapist, therefore her father is molesting her."

"It's not a leap in this case. I didn't exactly tell my mom about the pregnancy yesterday, but I totally begged her for anything in the grown-up channels that might be so awful that the kids never heard it. My mom's not a motormouth like Cecilly's mom, but I think she could see that Stacy was having trouble, and she confided something to me. She said the reason Mr. Kearney actually left was *not* that he'd found out about Mrs. Kearney's cheating. The husband's always the last to know, and supposedly Mr. Kearney is still clueless. It was that Mr. DeWinter had found him just outside the door of Stacy's bedroom a couple times in the middle of the night."

I froze as the vivid image of Mr. Kearney suddenly struck me. He had a slightly swollen beer gut, drooping mustache, muscular arms, and muscular neck. Add all that to the fact that he sometimes liked to go three days without shaving. And if he was out doing lawns, he could get that greasy, unwashed sweat all over his face. I couldn't remember the name of his lawn business on the T-shirts, but I could remember the slogan: PIT BULLS ARE BETTER THAN POODLES.

"I'm gonna throw up," Drew said. I guessed he was wide awake and sharing my mental pictures.

Lutz tapped his pen a couple times. I gathered this was new territory on an island where nothing ever happens. He finally uttered, "Did your mother say, um, where she got this information?"

"Yes. From Mrs. DeWinter."

"*Directly* from Mrs. DeWinter," he repeated, like that was important.

"Yeah. My mom's been keeping the books for the DeWinter Foundation since Mr. DeWinter had heart surgery last summer. She and Mrs. DeWinter have been spending a lot of time together. Mrs. DeWinter swore her to secrecy and said they had every family problem under control—including this one. I guess that means they threw Mr. Kearney out for that reason. But the secret's been driving Mom crazy. She loves Stacy, too, and when I started nagging her for info, it didn't take much to get it."

Lutz wrote and wrote. Something made me think that maybe he was stalling for time to think of questions in this mess. He inhaled, held his breath for a few strokes, then exhaled. "So Stacy didn't see a therapist for fear her grandfather would see the charge on the credit card and leap to what could be a wrong conclusion . . ."

Alisa nodded. "Yeah. So instead, we took her fifty bucks and twenty I had from waitressing that day, which is still far less than six visits to a shrink would cost, and we went to see Crazy Addy."

Lutz looked at her and dropped his chin into his hand.

"We walked in, and Crazy Addy took us upstairs to her kitchen, and Stacy said she needed to know the truth about something. And before we even sat down, Crazy Addy said, 'You've been raped.'"

Alisa raised her right hand slowly, staring at the captain. "All true. I swear."

He rolled his eyes, though his voice stayed as polite as possible. "And, uh . . . who did Ms. Gearta say was the, uh, culprit?"

"She didn't. I mean, not by name. Stacy babbled something about she might as well have gotten pregnant from a toilet seat, and Crazy Addy cut her off. She didn't laugh or anything. She just said, 'It is whom you suspect.' That was before I talked to my mom, so as far as I knew Stacy suspected *Mark*. We'd talked briefly about a date-rape drug. Stacy hadn't said much, but she didn't mention it as an impossibility in her mind. But when Crazy Addy said, 'It is whom you suspect,' Stacy screamed and ran out of there. But I've never asked her who it is. I can't. Stacy was a real basket case afterwards. If she wants me to know, she'll tell me. But still . . . *I* know who it is."

She and Lutz exchanged blinks and chimed, "You can just tell."

Alisa looked slightly amused beneath her sadness, but Lutz twisted his mouth up and muttered, "I hope you, um, didn't pay Ms. Gearta your hard-earned diner tips for that, um, forthcoming bit of logic, Alisa."

"But how'd she know Stacy was raped before we'd said anything but our names?"

"*Mm, mm, mm.*" He rolled his eyes. There could be a thousand answers to that.

Drew leaned forward, holding on to his stomach. He muttered at the glass, "Ask the *question*! Ask the question!"

Lutz came out of his glazed stupor and sat up straight. "I suppose we could sit here and speculate about Wally Kearney, and it would not give us proof of anything. I'm working on one crime here and need to solve it before I start in on any other. So despite all you've said, I have to ask you this: Did Stacy seem to you in a state of mind to shoot somebody?"

"Thank you," Drew muttered.

"Absolutely," Alisa said, which made Lutz raise his eyebrows in surprise, despite her little smile. "But not Casey Carmody. Stacy really doesn't have any problem with her. If Stacy wanted to hurt anybody in our crowd, it probably would have been Mark Stern. In spite of Casey, tonight he asked her to go back with him."

"Really?" Lutz wrote that down, letting nothing show

on his face to indicate that he'd heard the exact opposite version: Cecilly had reported that tonight *Stacy* had asked *Mark* to go back with *her*. Mark had told us the same thing.

I glanced at Drew, who looked puzzled.

Alisa laughed. "That's what kind of an idiot he is—he'll pop a question like that, with me right there in Stacy's house. He's too stupid to think I wouldn't be watching her back, right outside the door, if he asked to talk to her alone about something. Stacy had broken up with him because she was completely sick of his sex-on-the-brain routine. And here he was, going out with Casey Carmody and coming on to Stacy, as if that made him look like a knight in shining armor. She laughed in his face."

"You heard this yourself?"

"Plain as day. He said, 'I miss you. Don't you miss me? Why don't we do something about it and never say we did?'"

"You sure it wasn't the other way around? Her looking for a father in a moment of desperation? Without thinking?" Lutz hinted.

"Plain. As. Day. You can ask Stacy yourself."

"Do you know where she is?" he asked.

"She told me she was going home."

They exchanged stares.

I figured Stern was a big liar, but Alisa threw me off guard again. "Stacy said to Mark, 'If I were really Casey's friend, I would crank up my little rootin'-tootin' cowboy gun and put you out of your misery, lowlife. You're lucky I'm lukewarm on Casey these days.'"

"'Lukewarm'?"

"Well, Stacy and I started talking, in, like, April that we are suddenly lukewarm on all of our friends. Life around here just seems like a big bore."

I looked at Drew, and his eyes rolled to mine. Boredom seemed to be the Mystic Marvel plague.

"But that's what lukewarm *is*, Captain Lutz: lukewarm. You don't shoot a person because they suddenly seem dull and boring."

He tapped his pen on the table. "Why'd you tell Mark about the pregnancy?"

"I don't know anything about repressed memories. Truth? Yeah, I think that concept is way out there. But I kept getting back to the fact that Mark is so self-absorbed and stupid sometimes, maybe he used one of those date-rape drugs on her, the kind that you only have hazy memories afterward, if any. Stacy defends her dad all the time, almost as if to let me know she's really sure he didn't do anything to her. I can't stand the sight of the guy, but every once in a while I can get to believing her. Tonight? I believed her. I thought I would tell Mark, being that Stacy would die before showing she needed people. And as the father he ought to help Stacy make a decision. He's been irresponsible for too long. But I knew as soon as it was out of my mouth that it had been a brain flake."

"He didn't make any admissions?"

"No. In fact, he marched up to Stacy and called her a slut. I thought he was going to slap her. Then he told Cecilly Holst, just to get even, I guess. Put it this way: If he drugged Stacy and date-raped her, he wouldn't be running around telling the biggest gossips on the island that she is pregnant. He'd be begging for Stacy's silence and for the privilege of paying to terminate the pregnancy. Right?"

Lutz said nothing at first. He shook his head. "I don't know. I can't find a starting point tonight that helps make everything I'm hearing believable. You sound sincere, Alisa. But let me tell you something: Your story about a girl not remembering getting pregnant is like Noah not remembering he built the Ark. There's something wrong with the story. It was either a serious date-rape drug, or a serious, serious incest problem."

Alisa crossed her arms defensively. "And we're back to ground zero. There are things about Stacy even I don't know. And I know just about everything. I mean, it's no big deal for two best friends to talk about their romps with their Joes, even their mistakes with their Joes. Why would I care if Stacy took a quick break from her almighty Catholicism? I'm Protestant." She smirked but didn't smile. "Unless it's someone utterly raunchy and disgusting and beyond belief. I guess that's why I'm missing my beauty sleep to be here. I don't know anything about Casey Carmody. I didn't see anything. But someone needs to look into Mr. Kearney."

Lutz drummed his fingers on the table, nodding, and Alisa drummed hers on her arms. "Well then, tell me this, since I told you so much, Captain Lutz."

"I'll try."

"Does a girl who's being abused like that by her father ever go to crazy lengths to protect him?"

"Happens often," he said after a moment. "Lots of girls will continue to love their parents when their behavior is beyond belief. The girl feels responsible, feels like she's sending Daddy to jail. There's all sorts of motives like that."

She stood up slowly, rolling her eyes. "Okay then. Well, you solve it—after you solve this one. I'm just here to help Stacy. As for the pier, I heard and saw nothing . . . I never even heard a splash."

I got a chill again over that stupid splash. That *nonsplash.*

I barely paid attention, trying to imagine my sister treading water . . . or snoozing on a boat with her airhead face half into a pillow. Any image that made me think of her alive was good.

Alisa was talking again. ". . . when everyone up on the pier came running, at first I thought they were making it up. You know the stories these guys can tell about the ghosts and goblins wandering around up there. I thought this was some . . . Eddie Van Doren's ghost just fired his suicide pistol at Casey Carmody or something . . ."

Lutz caught my full attention by pushing his chair back with a *g-g-g-g-grunt.* "Well. Since we've got no body, no blood, and a whole lot of people claiming to have heard a pistol shot from a gun no one claimed to fire, you might not be too far off." Lutz stood up with a sarcastic smirk followed by a yawn.

I don't think he'd have smirked if he'd known what was coming his way next.

9

The surf club on Mystic is made up of three core guys, one core girl, and maybe a dozen other stragglers. They're not really a club in that they hold club meetings or do anything in an organized way. It's just that you might see a pack of eight or nine of them on the beach, or in the Pirates' Den, or in the surf shop, and that core of four was generally always there.

Lutz brought in the three guys at once, because somehow Indigo Somers hadn't come up onto the pier. The three guys made the room look kind of crowded. At the same time, it was odd to see Jon Hall, Ronny LaVerde, and Brin Olahano without Indigo and a crew of stragglers. They seemed like a body with an arm chopped off.

And they didn't look happy about being questioned,

either. They stood inside the doorway, kicking at the floor with their bare feet until Lutz said, "Take a seat."

"Dude, we don't know anything," Jon said with a polite but nervous laugh.

"Are you busting us again?" Ronny asked. He turned his pockets inside out with a pleading look.

"Because they've been good, both of them." Brin jerked his thumb down the row. "They've been going to meetings."

"Yes, I know." Lutz nodded hard.

"Wednesday we did Step Eight," Jon said pleadingly.

"And we were just *up there,* tonight, not doing anything we shouldn't on the pier. Except . . . being on the pier in the first place. Ha-ha!" Ronny laughed nervously.

"You know, we were just examining the stars and all," Jon said.

Drew muttered with a yawn beside me, "Huey, Dewey, and Louie," meaning that despite how Ronny was a blond and Brin was Hawaiian, these three were so much alike sometimes it could get confusing to listen to them. One thing the surf club was organized about was keeping their voice inflections the same. They all said "yah" instead of "yeah" and "bod" instead of "bad."

Lutz said, "Nobody's busted tonight. This is just friendly, just routine. Who knows? You might have seen something that you didn't know you saw."

"'Cuz the three of us were hanging out way off in the foundation of the old haunted house," Jon said. The Haunt was the first thing that burned to the ground up on the pier, but the metal girders were still in place. They worked like rusty benches.

"Look," Lutz said, rubbing the bridge of his nose, "something potentially very serious happened on that pier tonight. I'm not interested in anyone's marijuana escapades right now. I'm more interested in . . . what you observed on the pier."

"You mean, like, who was acting strange?"

"If anyone was, yes."

"The only strange sight I saw was Bill Nast." Jon gave a nervous giggle. "You wouldn't expect to see him at one of our parties. It's like a duck in a gaggle of seagulls. How's that? Good analogy?"

"But he wasn't doing anything. Bill's a good guy. He does my chemistry for me in school," Ronny added. "Ha-ha."

"Did you hear a shot fired?" Lutz asked them collectively.

"Yah."

"I heard it."

"Absolutely. But we didn't know it was a gun until people started running past us. It sounded like a . . . like a cap gun," Brin said.

"Did you see the gun?"

"No," Brin went on. "We heard later that a bunch of the Marvels were passing it around, but it never made it over our way. Carmody and Nast were standing a ways down from us. I think I saw Carmody give something small back to Mark Stern."

I heaved a little sigh of thanks, thinking Brin was one

witness for me in case Nast had slung his head up his butt and couldn't remember things right.

"Yah, that was all we saw," Ronny said.

"Did you hear anyone say who fired it?"

"They were pretty focused on getting off the pier and going down to the water to try to find Casey," Jon said. "Only thing I heard was that the gun belonged to Stacy Kearney."

"But Stacy gets a bum deal around here." Ronny nodded again.

"How do you mean?"

"People want to grind her up. It's hard to explain. You have to be like us . . ." Ronny made a circling motion to include his two friends. "You have to be on the outside looking in at the M&M's, but with a view close-up."

"The M&M's?" Lutz asked.

"Yah. The Mystic Marvels." Brin looked at his two friends, and they laughed a little. "Hey, we don't have much problem with the M&M's. We share the same beaches, same parties . . . When we get lucky, we even share the same babe pool. They're pretty nice—Kurt Carmody and those guys. They don't hassle us. But you kind of have to notice that some of those kids, they're, um, intolerant?"

"Intolerant how?"

Brin rubbed his forehead, like the exercise in hunting for words was tough. "Maybe *intolerant* is a bod word. That means, like, about gay people and Islamic people and all of that. For them it's just . . . *anybody.* And usually it's just one person, because they won't take on a crowd. But they'll, like, take on one of their own and totally annihilate that person, slowly but surely."

"Happens to somebody every year," Ronny put in. "I'd have been nervous seeing Billy Nast up there. But this season it's been Stacy Kearney so far. So I figured Bill was relatively safe. Ha-ha."

"Were people speaking ill of Stacy tonight that you heard?"

"Yah," Jon said. "They were like frothing curs over that Stacy is pregnant."

"And how did Stacy respond to this?" Lutz asked.

"She looked okay to me." Ronny shrugged. "She just came past like she was looking for somebody to talk to, and she stopped to joke with us for a minute."

"I totally felt, like . . . she was holding her head way up. Though maybe her head weighed a ton," Jon said. "Is that a good one? Ha-ha."

"What were you talking about with her?"

"Uh . . . we were talking about the moon," Jon said. "How it went behind this cloud, and the whole Mystic Marvels, like, disappeared. And you could only hear them, but they were like the ghost of Eddie Van Doren. All you could see was Casey Carmody's white sweatshirt. She looked like a huge white ghost in her bro's sweatshirt. Stacy, she just looked and said, 'How could a beautiful girl like Casey look so *el-huge-o*? That moon is not doing her justice.' Something like that. It wasn't totally funny, but we were cracking up with her. You had to be there."

Lutz kept writing.

"We didn't mention it, like, 'Yo, are you really pregnant?'" Brin said. "We just wouldn't do that. We figured, you know, that's her business."

"So then what happened?"

"She walked away and we, like, stuck our heads together kind of immediately." Brin grinned sheepishly. "We didn't want to hurt her feelings or anything. But we were wondering about this thing Mark Stern said to her on his way past to the ticket booth, which is the toilet. You know . . ."

"What did he say?"

"He said 'slut-cheater' to her on his way past. She flipped him the sign language. Two and two makes four, ya know? He wouldn't be calling her a slut-cheater if he was the dad, and she wouldn't be flipping him the bird if she wanted him as the father. So we came up with our own theory about who's the father."

"And what is that?"

The three of them looked at one another and cracked up.

"No . . ."

"No . . ."

"No. Uh-uh."

Lutz laid down his pen and rubbed at his eyes. His polite grin was starting to look petrified in place.

"I don't think it's going to help you find Casey Carmody," Brin said.

Lutz cleared his throat. "Well, why don't you let me decide that. There's every other officer on the force down on the beach and bay right now. It's my job to get some mileage out of you guys. Is your, um, theory based on something you saw?"

"Yah, lots of times. And it makes sense," Jon said, "though in a strange way."

"And what's weirder is there were six of us hanging out in my backyard after the coast guard told us to clear the water and quit trying to help. And, like, all at once, we *all* drew the same conclusion," Brin added, crossing his arms defensively.

"And all of us were clean and sober. Completely." Jon X-ed his T-shirt with his pinkie. "Well, all of us except one."

"Dude." Ronny glanced sideways at him in a disapproving way.

"Well, we're practicing Step Ten! Don't let any secrets back up on you," Jon argued.

"Yah, but Lutz doesn't need to know who wasn't sober, so long as it wasn't one of us!" He snapped his head around to face Lutz. "Right?"

Lutz let a stream of air out of his nose. "So long as it wasn't someone I've busted before."

"No," Jon said. "It was just Tito."

Tito Consuelez, I would almost say, is "core" in the surf club.

"He was all smoked up, but he was having a bod day. He lost his new board in the water," Jon said.

They watched Lutz write this down, and their eyes turned fearful.

"Don't be like that!" Jon begged him. "Tito just got the thing! It cost over five hundred dollars! His ankle strap came loose. The board must have gotten caught in a rip under the pier. I mean, we looked everywhere. He wasn't taking it so well—"

"On surfer beach? Just south of the pier?"

"Yah," they all chimed.

"We decided it was in Van Doren's Dungeon," Brin said remorsefully.

"I'll just make a note of it. If the coast guard comes up with a stray board, we'll call Tito and see if the ID matches. All right?"

They started to relax.

Van Doren's Dungeon refers to Eddie Van Doren and all the surfboards that have been lost under the pier during the summers. Rumor had it that his ghost rises out of the surf to steal some poor bastard's surfboard, and suck it down to some hell under the pier, aka Van Doren's Dungeon.

I'd say that on Mystic we'd always lost two boards a summer under the piers before Van Doren's suicide. The massive pilings that cause riptides and sea froth could occasionally suck a board. The board would seem to absolutely disappear. More surfboards *did* seem to disappear after Van

1

Doren's death—like, last year there had been four boards
lost. But the mature people on the island wrote the increase
off to the barrier islands chronically shifting and the surf
patterns changing. One board recovered a mile out by a
fishing trawler last summer didn't kill that Van Doren
rumor. Eddie Van Doren's ghost spit that one out, was all.

"With two choppers and two coast guard cruisers out
there, maybe Tito'll get lucky," Lutz said, reinforcing that
he wasn't interested in drug adventures. "So what's our big
theory? Can we relate this to who fired a gun and potentially hit Casey Carmody? Or is it just another dose of Mystic garble?"

They were all three quiet, except for a nervous laugh
or two.

"Captain Lutz, you just had to be there. You had to be up
on that pier at the half moon," Jon said, edging forward in
his chair. "The half moon shines with an eerie light, more
eerie than a full moon, because it plays more tricks. And
the stars get totally bright at the half moon. Like flashlights.
We were watching this . . . this just one little baby cloud that
came along slowly in front of the flashlight stars, and then
passed right over the half moon. Stacy was standing there
talking about Casey Carmody looking like a ghost in a bulky
white sweatshirt. It was like . . . a *prophecy* or something. Because two minutes later Casey Carmody totally disappears."

They all three shuddered, and I tried to ignore the spit
gathering in my mouth.

"I thought . . . you said Stacy Kearney gets a bum rap around here," Lutz muttered, not looking up from his paper. "Now you're implying she pulled the trigger?"

"No!" they exclaimed.

This time Ronny urged himself forward. "We were talking about Eddie Van Doren's ghost. And later it struck us—do you know when Eddie Van Doren died?"

Lutz sighed, as if he was expecting something I couldn't figure out. The date, being his first day as police captain, was so clear to him that he spouted it. "Sunday, September second—three years ago, Labor Day Weekend."

"Well, Indigo was in my backyard tonight, and we were all talking about this just as the police car came up," Jon said. "She pointed out that Stacy Kearney arrived on Mystic the day before school started their freshman year. She arrived *the day after* Eddie Van Doren died. Doesn't that strike you as odd?"

Lutz just watched with his chin in his palm and three fingers across his mouth. I thought he might be trying not to respond.

"The one way we've all described Stacy is . . . cold. Frigid. And nobody really knows her, knows much about her life before she got here. But a kid dies, and she shows up, right?"

Lutz sat frozen.

"Well, *what if* . . . What if *she's,* like . . . otherworldly?" Ronny asked quietly. "What if the father is Eddie Van Doren? What if it was Eddie Van Doren's gun that went off tonight? These are nice, peaceful people around here, Captain Lutz! They don't fire guns at each other! And since no one claims to have fired the gun on the pier—"

Brin jumped in "Maybe every few years Stacy and Eddie are going to find some beautiful young babe, or some promising young stud, and suck them down the hole into Van Doren's Dungeon with all the surfboards, until half this island is ghouls."

Lutz glanced at the ceiling, then dropped his pen on the table with a thud. My stomach was backing up, and after a moment I realized Drew was pulling at me, telling me to come away from this bullshit, that I wasn't in a good state of mind to hear it. But I was riveted, unable to tear my feet from the floor.

"Try to think of a better explanation!" Ronny encouraged him. "We've got a baby without a father, a girl who's always acted way too mysterious, almost like . . . *she's haunted*. We have a gunshot without a shooter, and now . . . a missing girl who everyone saw fall off the pier. And then nobody heard a splash! I can't tell you exactly where she is, Captain Lutz. But I'll tell you this much—I don't think you're ever going to find her."

Lutz stood up slowly, and without meeting their eyes said, "I will try, gentlemen. Thank you for your time."

I let Drew pull me along to the public areas. Yeah, it was time for a break.

10

Drew and I didn't go into the back lobby, where it sounded like a smaller bunch of kids were still waiting. I thought I heard Cecilly's voice, which wouldn't have surprised me. The gossips wouldn't leave until the last drop of intrigue had been drunk. We went outside and rested our backs against the huge concrete lions that were supposed to make some sort of a statement about our "roaring" police force.

The night was still, save for the far-off drone of choppers. If I looked southeast, I could barely make out the glow above what must have been a dozen searchlights.

"I want to go back down to the beach," I said, but Drew shook his head.

"Please don't."

He wouldn't look up, wouldn't look at me. I looked at my watch. 4:09. In another hour, my cell phone would ring, the cops would answer it, then hand it to me. It was looking very much like I would have nothing good to tell my parents.

"I just don't know how I can tell my mom and dad that I hadn't even been checking the beach myself," I said.

"That's the last thing they'd want you to do."

He was implying that at this hour it was more likely that I would stumble on something that would haunt me forever. I just wanted to holler my brains out. Watching these interviews turn from weird to unbelievable kept my mind busy, but not my fried gut. It was screaming that Jon, Ronny, and Brin were not so far off. You start realizing that your sister is probably dead, you don't need to add ghouls. Your horror is just as complete without them.

I started to think really strange things—thoughts that still kind of circled around the here and now without landing on it, but they were getting pretty close. I started seeing myself trying to explain my life to someone after going to college where no one knew me:

"You got brothers or sisters?"

". . . I had a sister but she died."

"Wow, I'm sorry. Was it sudden, or was she sick?"

"It was sudden . . . We think she drowned. But she might have got smoked by one of our friends. We don't know, we never found her—"

I jumped out of my skin as the double doors burst open, and Ronny, Jon, and Brin flew with their freedom. When they saw me, though, it was like a three-car pileup, and they came right over, looking awkward as shit. I didn't want to jump on them for making my sister into a Van Doren's Dungeon myth before the sun had even come up. I didn't want to jump on anyone for anything at this point. Things get this serious, and you're like a sponge that's been wrung out. Your brains are kind of damp but not taking on anything and not giving off anything. It's a safe feeling— being able to have some damp thoughts . . . being beyond tired, beyond horrified, beyond frantic, beyond outraged. I stared at three sets of feet in front of me, three sets of sunburned bare feet showing white *V*s from three sets of Reefs, reminding me that this was an island where the sun came out regularly and burned people's feet.

Brin brought his hand up slowly and then patted the back of my neck. "Dude. I would offer you, like, a pop from the pop machine. But I don't have any money on me. We got *nabbed*, totally by surprise, from Jon's house."

It was the perfect way to talk about the situation, I guessed, kind of sideways. They were neither hitting on nor dodging the issue.

I muttered, "I'm okay."

"No, you're not. I got money . . ." Jon reached in his surfer shorts pocket. "You want soda, Kurt? Help you stay awake."

"Thanks, but . . ." I remembered that Jon smoked cigarettes. I could see the pack in his T-shirt pocket, and I reached for it and took one. He lit it. I could feel Drew's eyes all over me. He had no idea I ripped off my dad's pack maybe once every couple weeks . . . enjoyed a butt on the beach when life looked overwhelming. I felt entitled right now.

Jon lit it quickly and said nothing, grateful, I sensed, for something he could do.

Ronny reached around his own neck, unhooked his surfer necklace, and put it around my neck. "It's for luck," he said. "Saved my neck on more than a few bodass waves."

I'd seen Ronny wearing that thing since time began. The three of them were squirming kind of awkwardly, maybe their own words about my sister still echoing through their heads.

"I wish this were happening to somebody besides you," Brin said. "Why does shit like this always happen to the nicest people?"

The nasty thought did rush through my head: *If I were the pope himself and I drowned out there, I don't suppose that would stop people from making a pier spook out of me.* But instead I took a long drag on the cigarette, trying to get accustomed to the thought that people could be making your sister out to be the next island sea hag behind closed doors and telling you how nice you are to your face. Ronny sounded really sincere both times. Somehow I gathered that he was.

They trotted off slowly, promising to be at the other end of their cells if I needed anything. I exhaled up to the half moon, which was sinking toward the southern horizon.

Drew looked at the moon, glancing sideways to watch me smoke. He grinned sleepily. "Getting your last twitch of freedom before school takes it all away?"

Ah yes, the ill-fated Naval Academy. I looked down at the cigarette, which really tasted like shit. I didn't understand how my dad could do this to himself first thing every morning. But it did wake me up a little. It took an hour and a half off my tiredness.

I tried to get my ribs to expand out of their iron state, and I said, "I don't think I'm going."

Drew watched me, kind of frozen. "You're not serious. You're just a little nuts right now. You'll feel normal again after they find Casey."

Normal. I wondered what that was. I wondered if it was normal to stick to the same places, same friends, same stupid nightly bullshit when I'd been left with nothing but the dull taste of stale smoke over the things we did, the things we talked about, for at least six months. I wondered if it was normal to be beyond your senior year in high school and still chatting it up about ghosts and a couple of suicides up on the pier. The only times I'd really felt *normal* recently were when I was Fog6767. I surely didn't feel normal now that my sister was missing.

"I won't feel *normal,*" I told Drew. "I haven't been that in a while."

It took him a respectful minute to ask, "What do you mean?"

I almost wished he'd asked right away. It would have been more trusting, more . . . *whimsical.* I told myself I was nitpicking, and he was only trying to say the right thing. But *whimsical,* odd word that it was, came to me as something I was totally lacking around here. I felt like I was in a straitjacket.

"I just feel like . . . everybody around me is about ten feet off," I blathered, trying to feel gratified over this blast of truth. "I can't . . . get right up to anyone. I just feel very, very . . . weird inside. I feel different."

"I think we all feel weird inside," Drew said hesitantly. "My theory? It starts with the first time you make use of your five girlfriends. You're weird forever after." He wagged his five fingers in the air.

I couldn't remember the first time I'd found my "five girlfriends." I was young. It hadn't been any big deal. How's that for weird?

I was two hundred blog posts ahead of Drew. I didn't know where to start with catching him up. I resented the fact that I had to find a starting point with a guy who was supposed to be my best friend, on this night of all nights. But if I was honest, I couldn't blame Drew. He not only accepted everything I said, but he also admired a lot of it. I could have found the words. I had chosen not to.

"The stupid newspapers, they're my biggest problem," I said, taking a long drag on the cigarette and pushing thoughts of Casey backward again. "You realize it's been printed sixty thousand times that you're going to the Naval Academy, and you're seeing your face splashed underneath the banner *Atlantic City Press, Lifestyle Section*—you feel like your throat is shut."

"You *really* don't want to go?" he asked.

"I want to . . . *not* want to *not* go. I don't know what the hell is up with me."

I don't know what I expected him to say. His silence was normal, but when I got it, I realized it was more than the newspapers closing my throat off. I just decided to throw it all out there for Drew. It was a stupid thought, but smart thoughts hadn't helped in any way tonight.

"I've been blogging all summer. Sometimes, I'm talking about the academy, trying to figure out why I don't want to go. Other times I'm just this . . . faceless, identityless guy, and I talk about all kinds of shit."

"Like what?" he asked, but with just the right second of pausing. It was, like, obligatory, like there was no part of my best buddy that looked for an original reply.

I tried not to sigh. There was no part of me that could actually say the worst of it. I was totally bored one night in June, and I got this thought in my head: *I wonder what girls feel like? I wonder if they feel different from us, in spite of all this talk about everyone being the same?* And I had wandered about on the Internet as Helga474, telling people on weight-loss sites that I was this totally blimped-out girl who hadn't gone to her prom. I got some responses. I answered them. I mean, for a day it was totally a rip to be Helga474. But do I tell this to Drew? Nuh-uh. He would think I was gay, and it had nothing to do with being gay. It had to do with being totally bored and kind of curious in a place where breaking rules doesn't really matter. Jesus, there were so many rules around here.

"You can't be too fat, too skinny, too tall, too short, too smart, too dumb, too loud, too quiet around here . . ." I blathered. "You can't be too anything. It's against the rules. Do you realize that?"

"Is this, like, chapter two of seeing all your friends in black-and-white?" Drew asked with enthusiasm. He liked to hear me blather, so long as I didn't get too crazy with it.

"Black-and-white was a couple months ago. Right now? I'm starting to see *through* people. They're evaporating."

"Nice," he said, but not sarcastically. "I always thought it was just us—until tonight. Seems like a lot of them are feeling it, ya know, this thing where it's time to . . . move on. But what do you do? We'll be out of here in less than two months. We'll all get back together every summer, and it'll be cool. It's been cool, the Marvels are cool. You just need a break, is all. I think we all do."

I just didn't know if a break was all I needed. And *cool* seemed like a dirty word all of a sudden. Mucky, dingy, irritatingly lukewarm. What about hot or cold? What about scalding or freezing? I felt like I needed to turn completely inside out, do something outrageous. I didn't know what, but going to military school seemed not outrageous . . . just prestigious. There was a big difference, I realized. Maybe it was the rush of nicotine, but my thoughts revved up too clearly.

"Drew, you know what a Mystic Marvel is? It's someone who has sold everything about themselves that is a little bit different. The girls we hang with are very decent to look at, and we do all the right stuff . . . all the normal sports, all the expected stuff . . . We excel at normalcy. We're the world's greatest—what's the word?—*conformists*. We are the people who can sell our souls the best. Congratulations. We're marvy all around. We'll end up like Mark Stern, with nothing that feels stunning except sex, so we'll end up with pricks for brains. We can't find anything about ourselves that we like after we've sold everything off, so we feel this strange twitch to go into a Jesus factory. True *needs* a Jesus factory right now—if you gotta get your exoticness back! It's no wonder we're so obsessed with ghosts and ghouls and suicides on the pier. It takes one to know one! I want to be—" I was pretty exhausted and crazed and looking for something dramatic. "I would rather be a drag queen than what I am. A nothing. A haunt. A spook."

It occurred to me that of all the Mystic Marvels, only one was a little bit different: a little too rich, a little too poor, a little too giving, a little too mean, a little too well dressed, a little too prone to potty mouth. Stacy Kearney stuck out, not for any totally awful reasons, but she stuck out for a number of them. Suddenly she was on trial all over town for murder.

"You're not nothing, dude," Drew told me, trying to be nice, trying to help me along with this exercise in not thinking about my sister for just a few minutes. My rant fest hadn't really helped anything. I'd got a load off my chest, but I still had huge decisions to make. There was no way to make them tonight, so talking about them had seemed like what it was—an exercise in pretending they are the worst problems

I had. They had seemed so important until tonight. They were about my almighty social status, which was suddenly so annoying. I had the stray thought again that Captain Lutz had no idea who had fired the gun, and even I was a suspect. I wondered if I'd get arrested for attempted murder. And I thought at least that would be something hot or cold . . . not something so goddamned coooooooool. . . .

 **11**

A car door slammed at the curb. I looked up to see the island's only Bentley. I found myself rising to my feet as Stacy's grandparents came up the walk. Mr. DeWinter had a package in his hand, like a good-sized bubble envelope, that drew my curiosity. But I took a step backward instinctively as they came within ten feet, probably because I didn't know what to say. Their granddaughter was being accused left and right of shooting a gun at my sister. On the one hand I knew them as the center force of charity to the grown-ups on this island. I felt off balance, to put it mildly.

Mr. DeWinter wore a strained expression, like the folds around his eyes had swollen and hardened, and now they kept his eyes open more than shut. He limped a little, and I couldn't quite tell whether the problem was his legs or his spine. He came right over, and he shook my hand and squeezed my arm.

"Don't give up hope," he said. "I just called the coast guard office in Philadelphia—pulled some strings through a navy admiral who served under me in the sixties. They're sending down two additional choppers to search the down-seas."

"Thank you . . . very much," I said numbly.

I wanted to go on about how much I appreciated that, but I was a little frozen by his breathing. It sounded kind of labored and exhausted. It did strike me what a feat it was for him to think of my family's problems when he had so many of his own. I supposed it was to his advantage to find Casey alive, though his presence of mind and his ease with facing me blew me away. He'd gotten used to being under fire for years, thanks to Stacy's mom and all her bad behavior. I noticed she hadn't come.

His eyes tore to the double doors. "Let's get this taken care of," he said over his shoulder, and his wife followed him into the lobby.

I watched their backs until they disappeared.

Drew let out a sigh. "We're not going back in there. Believe me, you don't need to hear the DeWinters."

"Why not?" I asked, feeling like I didn't have a brain left to make decisions with.

"You'll get frustrated. The DeWinters are like the Generous Good Fairies around here, and that's real nice and everything, but you probably won't hear a word about your sister. This is about to turn into The Stacy Show."

I figured I'd been hearing The Stacy Show all night, anyway. But if Drew was right, the adoring grandparents would be totally focused on clearing her name. No, I didn't have the endurance to sit through all of that. I almost went back to my initial urge to go to the beach.

I looked down there. I thought I could hear a chopper far off, but I realized the beach was suddenly dark. The spots were gone. Maybe Drew had been alert to that detail while I was blathering, and he hadn't wanted to say anything.

"They're pulling out, aren't they?" I asked. "They're giving up."

"The crew probably just went home to get a couple hours' rest," he said. "They can only do so much in the dark. They'll be back at first light."

My heart fell into my gut, and Drew grabbed my arm, probably in case I decided to run down there. I didn't get the chance.

Drew's dad pulled up in his chief's car, and four very tired-looking cops piled out. Chief Aikerman came over and tried to hug me, tried to tell me in his calmest voice that Casey could be somewhere on the island; she could be treading water in the down-seas, but they'd have better luck finding her out there at first light.

"I wanna go down to the beach. I need to see for myself," I said urgently.

"It's pitch-black, Kurt," he argued, pointing at the half moon, which loomed over the horizon of Atlantic City. "Look, I'm not giving up, so I don't want to see you give up. Sun'll be back in an hour and a half. Besides, if you're not here when your parents call, that will be . . . not good. Think of them. They need to hear one of their children's voices."

Aw, bullshit, I wanted to say. They could give me back my phone, trust me not to stand there and pick my boogers if my sister tried to call . . . but I could tell it was pointless to argue. The other cops spoke to me nicely, then went for their own cars, and Chief Aikerman said, "The DeWinters are here?"

Drew jerked his head at their Bentley. "They came to get Stacy out of hot water, I guess. She's in some, in case you haven't heard. I'll say no more."

"I'm aware," his dad said, and disappeared inside. I supposed he was being kept apprised of everything while on the beach.

I felt torn up about Stacy. If she had an incest problem in the family, I felt sorry for her because that was terrible— but I really didn't want to hear about it. Not before my sister was found. But I turned toward the inside of the station, anyway, scuffing my feet like a zombie. With Stacy's life unfolding like some sort of horror movie, I felt like I ought to try to accept that she could have shot at my sister. After all, everyone else I'd heard tonight thought she was guilty. If I couldn't get to the beach, the least I could do was face the truth of what happened. I could listen to the DeWinters and read between the lines.

Drew followed as I sneaked past the doorway to the back lobby, and we took the hallway back around to the window.

Sure enough, Chief Aikerman was in there, so we didn't have to worry about being caught. Mr. DeWinter was still a pretty muscular guy. He had a swarthy, self-confident way of walking around, and it reminded me that fifty years ago he had gone to West Point. There were no Naval Academy graduates on the barrier islands, so when my acceptance was formally announced at the spring awards assembly at school, the principal had picked Mr. DeWinter to give me Coast Regional's 44th Dream Big Award.

The lights on the school stage were blinding, and I'm a fish out of water on a stage, so I barely remember anything except that the applause reminded me of battlefield gun-shots—and that Mr. DeWinter's handshake had been grip-ping to the point of being painful. He was one of the people I thought of when I pictured myself telling folks I wasn't going to the Naval Academy. In the Mystic Museum, half of which was early island photos from the DeWinter estate, were also his Vietnam medals, his Vietnam guns, his grand-father's World War I guns, his great-grandfather's Civil War pistol, and a couple of swords that dated back to the fam-ily's arrival here from England in the 1700s. He would just never understand my decision. Maybe he'd post a big sign in the museum with my photo on it, just under the words: MYSTIC MORON.

For the moment I could make out confusion and suffering in his eyes. They darted, and his brow was drawn in, and the way he breathed was actually scary. He kept making an O shape out of his mouth after he sat down, and he would blow his breath out through it like that was helping him keep a steady heart.

I glanced at Drew, who was shaking his head. "If he kicks the bucket over his kids and grandkids, they all better haul it back up to Connecticut and never show their faces around here again," he whispered.

Mrs. DeWinter seated herself beside him, patting his back and gazing at Lutz.

"Chief, why don't you go home and get some sleep?" Mr. DeWinter said in his amazingly gallant way. "You'll have to be back at it at first light—"

"I'm going, Cliff. I just wanted to stop in and say I really appreciate your coming down here. I'm sure you've got enough problems." He stood up and said, "Also, I don't want the Carmody kid to see me leave. I don't want *him* leaving, and being among the missing when his folks call, but . . ."

He turned to go and I almost laughed. *Podunk island . . . How in hell can the chief of police forget what he'd taught his son about this room?* I grabbed Drew's arm to draw him back outside, thinking his dad would remember any second and come around to check on our whereabouts. We needed to be out front again.

But Drew said, "He'll go out the back to check his desk

first. If he doesn't, we'll see him go past the window in the door."

So I just stood there amazed as the window stayed clear. I think Chief Aikerman is a good chief of police—as far as maintaining order goes on islands where little happens. But the fact that the cops could be so electronically lame made me wonder about other things . . . like if they were psychologically lame, too. They probably had a better shot at finding my sister than understanding what had happened to Stacy in her house.

I watched Mr. DeWinter intently.

"Of course, my primary intent is to clear Stacy's name of any wrongdoing, but we'll take things in any order that's helpful to you."

Drew nudged me to let me know he had correctly named this The Stacy Show.

Lutz picked up his pen yet again. "First off, you must have heard by this time that there's a rumor floating around that Stacy bought a small handgun. Were you aware of that?"

"Yes, I was," he said to my amazement. He brought the bubble envelope out of his lap, took his time unfolding the flaps, and pulled out a document and handed it to Lutz.

"Gun license . . . ," Lutz mused, looking the document over, "with your name on it."

Mr. DeWinter then handed him an envelope that looked like it would hold a card. " 'For Granddaddy,' " Lutz read, and stared at them in confusion. "So . . . you're saying that Stacy purchased it . . . as some sort of gift?"

"My birthday is August first. I do have a collection, which of course I keep at the museum and not in the house. Believe me, I was unhappy about the purchase. Especially when I found it in her dresser drawer last week, *not* under lock and key. I told her she might be of legal age, but I don't think an eighteen-year-old ought to be making presents out of guns—for just this reason. Something unusual happens on the island, and *Boom!*—the blame falls in the wrong place."

Lutz handed the license back, watching the DeWinters. "And where is the gun?"

"At this moment we don't know," he confessed. "Around midnight I unlocked my desk to get out my heart medicine, and I noticed then it was missing. I thought maybe Dorothy had moved it . . ." He jerked his head at his wife. "Unfortunately, I've been having more problems with my ol' ticker this spring. I thought my angioplasty last summer had resolved all of that. At any rate, I'm not as sharp with my ears and eyes as I used to be. I don't know when it was taken or by whom. It might even have been yesterday."

His heart was probably giving way over the Kearneys' divorce, I thought, and I wondered if Stacy's mom could do anything except suck the life out of the people around her. And the father? I had no words.

"So someone took the gun?" Lutz asked.

"Someone took the gun." He nodded unhappily. "I should have had it sent down to the museum the first day I saw it. I don't know what I was thinking. However, don't lose sight of the point here. Stacy had a normal and sane reason to buy such a thing—as a gift, not as a weapon to do damage to anyone, least of all to another young person."

It helped a little, but not all that much, I felt. Stacy obviously had something to do with the gun ending up at the pier. She probably had known where the key to the desk was. "Here's one question I have: A half dozen kids have walked through here tonight, claiming to have been in the McDonald's one night when Stacy and her boyfriend said jokingly that she had bought a gun. If it were simply an antique and a gift for Grandpa, why not just say so?"

"Stacy can be . . . very flamboyant." Mr. DeWinter defended her, "It's a thing I love about her, but at times it has a downside. I could see her not admitting it just to . . . have an audience."

"Let me reword that . . ." Lutz shuffled around like the answer didn't satisfy him. "Could the gift element be an excuse? Could Stacy have bought a gun because she thought she needed, um, protection from someone?"

"He wants to ask about Mr. Kearney . . . ," Drew muttered, "find out if it could be true, and find out if Stacy was unstable enough to fire the thing at someone."

I glanced at my watch, figuring I would never follow this. 4:26.

When I looked back Mr. DeWinter was doing a bunch of his O-shaped exhales. "Lutzie . . . I wasn't going to bring Wally into this tonight. He obviously has nothing to do with the missing Carmody girl, and we expect that you need to solve that immediately. The missus and I, we can handle what comes our way."

"I understand that, but I need to know. There may be a second crime here that needs looking into, and one might have to do with the other." Lutz forced himself to look up. "I need to know what the deal is with Wally's . . . character. Anything you know."

Mr. DeWinter dipped his head and brought it back up tiredly. But he said point-blank, "We . . . don't have any proof."

Ker-blam! Nothing said, but it all hung in the air. I could barely look.

Mrs. DeWinter spoke up. "My husband found Wally just outside of Stacy's bedroom on two separate occasions."

Her wide eyes looked bewildered, and I tore my eyes down to the floor again. Mrs. DeWinter had always come across to me as a sweet little old lady—not a rocket scientist by any means. You'd probably think that she wouldn't even know about stuff like this. "It was after the second time that Clifford told Wally to pack his bags."

Lutz raised his eyebrows at Mr. DeWinter, who only shrugged. "Of course, I suspect something. I suspected after the first time—his and Sam's bedroom is in the other wing of the house! But the first time Stacy merely said that he had walked in his sleep and she had woken him up."

Lutz rubbed his forehead with two fingers. "Please tell me you didn't believe that."

"I didn't, but Stacy swore up and down he didn't do anything to her, so I guess I'm naive. I expect every man out there to be a straight shooter like I am. The second time I found him outside her door, he was packed and out of the house by morning. I know now I should have done it the first year they came. I might still have a good heart. Maybe Samantha could have dated openly, maybe changed her tastes a little. I just . . . thought that if I kept turning the other cheek, one day the man would stop hating us. He hated us from the first day he met Samantha, and it just never got any better. Jealousy does strange things."

He laughed so sadly, with the same befuddled look as Mrs. DeWinter. "The world's a mysterious place sometimes, Lutzie. If you can tell me how Wally wielded so much influence over two strapping boys, and yet their grandmother and I can do nothing right . . . I'll never question anything else in my life."

Lutz sat rooted and stared at the couple almost defensively. "Is Sam's face covered in scratches right now?"

"Yes," Mr. DeWinter admitted, and watched Lutz in even more confusion. "Don't tell me . . . Stacy's being blamed for that, too?"

"Can you tell me how it happened?"

"Samantha didn't say . . ." His voice got so soft it scared me. "We assumed it was a boyfriend, but we can find out for you. Listen, we're not stupid. We know Sam's been dating for quite some time. We simply couldn't blame her, being that her choice of a husband had not been, er, good. I had hoped her regrets would improve her taste. I cannot say that has happened."

"But . . . scratching someone in the eyes? That's a lady's fight," Lutz said. "That's not a boyfriend."

"Well, maybe there was a jealous third party." Mr. De-Winter shrugged, making his O-shaped mouth a couple times. "Samantha is still quite striking. No one can deny that. And— "

"It *was* Stacy." Mrs. DeWinter's eyes rose from the table again. She glanced sideways at her astonished husband, then met Lutz's gaze. "I . . . I was there. I saw the end of it."

Mr. DeWinter's voice was still low . . . maybe from weakness, I thought. "You . . . kept that from me?"

"Because of your heart, Clifford." Mrs. DeWinter laced her fingers through her husband's with one hand, and brushed a tear from her eye with the other. "When I walked in on it, Stacy had her mother backed into the corner. She was crying and screaming, 'You should have protected me! You're my mother!'"

The room got deadly silent except for Mrs. DeWinter's occasional sniffs and Mr. DeWinter's blowing exhales.

Mr. DeWinter finally muttered, "Oh my god."

Lutz forced himself on anyway, in a tone that sounded almost like that of a father talking to small children. "I just have to wonder, Clifford, if the birthday present for you wasn't a ruse. Could she have, in some convoluted teenage way, thought that she was protecting herself—"

"Protecting us all, maybe?" Mr. DeWinter rested his head on his fingertips. "I had thought of that. Despite Stacy's flamboyant streak, the purchase of a gun . . . for a gift . . . It always seemed a little nonsensical, since all my guns are kept at the museum. Maybe she felt that her father would break back in . . . hurt someone while drinking . . . She's so loyal to family. She would do anything for us."

And for friends? I thought of my sister in the halo again, wondering what had come over me. I ought to be more ready to hang the girl than anyone. But I still felt the vibrations of a big-time railroad going on here. Maybe I was stupid, but that's what I felt.

Lutz looked at them, more than slightly annoyed. "Why not prosecute?"

"Prosecute Wally?" Mrs. DeWinter sat forward in her bewildered way. "Because Stacy insists her father never touched her."

"The victims don't always need to testify. You could get her to talk to a shrink, and the shrink could testify."

"We asked her to see Dr. Holst and she refused. Hasn't Stacy been forced through enough?" Mrs. DeWinter came to life again.

I remembered True's story about the cell-phone spying, and how Dr. Holst hadn't been on the list of shrinks Stacy had tried to call. I gathered they had no idea how much their granddaughter thought she *should* see a shrink. Sometime, when this night was long, long behind us, I wanted to sit with my dad and ask him hours of questions. It seems like in families with this big a secret, so many things never get said. Stacy was a hotbed of secrets—secrets she kept from her own family as well as from us.

Mrs. DeWinter continued, "Captain Lutz, we might not look like good citizens in this case. But we are good family people. We have to think of our granddaughter first. We offered Wally quite a settlement after we found this gun, if he would simply leave Mystic, leave Stacy's haven, so she can run the beaches freely, go about with her friends, and be a kid! We could prosecute him, in Connecticut, as soon as she has time to think and breathe! That's all we want. Call it Grandma's instinct, but I don't think Wally has a . . . a thing for young girls in general. I think it's specific to our granddaughter."

"That's a dangerous assumption," Lutz said.

"I agree with my wife," Mr. DeWinter said. "When I offered him the settlement, he said, 'I'm not leaving without Stacy!' Isn't it true that certain pedophiles feel their love for the victim is, er, sacred or something?"

Mr. DeWinter went on in a wheezing rant, "Stacy has been through a lot. But no matter what she's been through, she would not buy a gun and plan to shoot a young person.

No matter what happened at the pier, I'm sure she did not pull the trigger on her friend."

Lutz cleared his throat, and I held on to the window ledge as he dropped the bomb. "Did you know that Stacy's pregnant? And that the boyfriend is denying paternity?"

They sat totally frozen, and I couldn't hear Mr. De-Winter even breathe until he finally sucked in the biggest gulp of air yet. I turned my back.

"I can't hear this. I can't watch this," I blathered. I held on to my stomach as Drew spoke up.

"I don't get it. Didn't Mr. Kearney move out in *January*? So how . . ."

"I don't know," I said, though the unanswered questions banged through my head. Alisa had just sworn that Stacy couldn't remember any rape . . . So why would she buy a gun over something she couldn't remember? Was she just saying she couldn't remember because it was too hard to confirm to someone? Because she felt responsible? Could she have visited her father? At the yacht club, Mark had said he'd called her once and heard her brothers arguing in the background. Why would a girl go visit her father, and her brothers who stood behind him, if he would do something like that? Nothing made sense, and something told me that a lot of this never would. I glanced at my watch again stupidly. 4:31.

"We'll get the pregnancy terminated. First thing tomorrow." Mr. DeWinter's voice came through more strongly than I would have imagined.

"Do you know where she is?" Lutz asked.

"She didn't come back to the house tonight," Mr. De-Winter muttered.

"Do you mind if we search your place?" Lutz asked.

"Of course not. Anything that helps . . ."

I turned as a seat roared backward. Mr. DeWinter was on his feet, having turned toward the door. Mrs. DeWinter stood up, too, and though I'd predicted it, I was not ready to see it—Mr. DeWinter suddenly dropped. Mrs. DeWinter raced for him.

"Jeezus, that is so unjust," Drew muttered as I turned my back again. I even put my fingers in my ears to cover the sounds of Mrs. DeWinter calling her husband's name. Their family embarrassments went back thirty years, supposedly. The camel's back was breaking.

"Closeness of where they keep the ambulance will probably save him," Drew muttered. He was looking over my shoulder, and I heard Lutz talking to the paramedic squad, which kept its ambulance directly across the street at the firehouse. "But I almost hope . . . it doesn't save him."

I watched Drew look guiltily through the glass. He said, "I was just . . . being a little selfish here. And a little crazy, too. I keep hearing Crazy Addy bellowing, saying she could feel someone's heartache and anguish, and that person would die close to morning."

I shut my eyes and couldn't hold back a half-baked smirk. "Jeezus, we are losing it, bro." It seemed to me Crazy Addy had babbled about a "she," not an old man, but

Drew's confusion between reality and myth backed up on me, too.

"The guy's old. He's lived his life." Drew laughed nervously.

I didn't argue.

But by the time the paramedics were in the room with Mr. DeWinter, he was already sitting up, refusing an oxygen mask. He looked very gray, but very alert. Not near death.

Before Lutz could bail on the questioning to end up in the ambulance with Mr. DeWinter, one of the deputies came through. He said they'd found Stacy Kearney. Wally Kearney had been speeding off of Mystic in her Audi. When a cop pulled him over, they'd found Stacy in the trunk of the car. The officers, knowing they had just saved Stacy, were not watching her as they arrested Wally. She had taken off into the night.

But they had Wally Kearney in the chief's office, in handcuffs.

12 🌀

I don't know what came over me—maybe that fight-or-flight syndrome my dad's always writing into his Mike Atlas stories. But I turned and followed the little corridor around to the bigger one and stalked into the back lobby. I was going to punch this guy's lights out.

Drew must have sensed my growing anger, because he was grabbing at me again and saying, "Don't get stupid . . . you're exhausted, is all."

"I gotta do something! I *am* exhausted from standing around and doing nothing, that's all! He started all of this—"

If it hadn't been for her father, Stacy wouldn't have gotten twisted up enough to buy a gun. It wouldn't have ended up on the pier, and my sister and I would be home sleeping

right now. I felt like I was being torn in half all of a sudden—
half of me was worried for my sister and half for Stacy.

Things are not always the way they look. And though it
looked like Stacy tried to hurt my sister, something inside of
me was still insisting that was all too easy.

"Let's pick on the rich kid that everyone hates," I muttered with sarcasm, and tried to get Drew off my arm.
"Think they'd be so busy hating her if they knew what we
know?"

"I don't think this has anything to do with the fact that
she's rich," Drew argued.

"Am I the only person on this goddamned island with
any imagination?" I yelled. "Give me an ending I couldn't
predict, please!"

I said it so loud that Drew backed off. But the police
had their own yelling match going on, so no one was paying much attention. All the kids were finally gone, and Mr.
Kearney was alone with Little Jack outside Chief Aikerman's office. I don't know where the arresting officers were,
but Mr. Kearney was having a loud say.

"—ain't telling you nothing! I want a lawyer! And I
want you to tell those two . . . Neanderthals who brought
me in to go find my kid that they scared off!" With his
hands cuffed, he was pointing his index fingers toward
Little Jack's chest. But he dropped into a chair as Lutz came
out of the questioning room.

"Gee, that's funny, Wally." Lutz moved to the coffeepot

with some crazed, exhausted laugh. "I don't suppose she was at all scared by being in the trunk of the car!"

"I ain't saying nothing." Mr. Kearney looked down, and I suddenly wondered at the value of punching out a guy with a pissed-off cop and an exhausted police captain surrounding him. I came toward him, though. I think I was going to grab him by the collar and shake his head loose. But he looked up and pointed both fingers at me.

"I'll tell you where she is . . . she's off trying to find *his* sister! She decided she wouldn't leave until the Carmody girl was found. So me and my sons, we stuffed Stacy in the trunk. She was leaving now, tonight, with me and her brothers. That was what the four of us decided at midnight, so—"

"You trash heap—" I reached for him, but Lutz was faster and got me in some kind of a strong hold without even spilling his coffee. I managed to say, "Stacy wouldn't go anywhere with you!"

"Split 'em up, Jack!" Lutz roared, and I supposed he meant for Little Jack to take Mr. Kearney into the other room, but Mr. Kearney still wasn't budging from his chair.

"Wait, Lutzie!" Mr. Kearney looked from him to me. "The kid's sister is missing . . . he's gotta be half-crazed. I ain't talking to you, but I'll talk to *him*. My daughter likes him! Let him go! He ain't gonna do nothing to me."

I wondered how he knew so much, and I wondered what he meant by "My daughter likes him." I had only seen

Mr. Kearney—and had barely said hello to him—the times I saw him at Stacy's house over the years. But he had seemed to recognize me pretty quickly.

Lutz loosened his grip slowly. Maybe he thought he could get some information this way. He held on to my arm as Little Jack pulled a chair up so I was facing Mr. Kearney, but from about six feet away. "Wally, if you say one thing to upset this kid, I will find something to add to the lengthy list of charges we got going now—"

Mr. Kearney stared at me, but he laughed. "Gee, I'm so frightened. I wasn't even speeding. What have you got on me?"

"You *were* speeding . . . that's why you got stopped."

"That's a crock—you recognized Stacy's car."

"Driving a stolen vehicle, attempted kidnapping . . . We'll stop there for the time being."

Lutz must have thought I didn't know about the worse crimes or that I was staring at a complete pig. I supposed this was part of the ending I could never have guessed— that I'd be sitting across from a child molester who was try- ing to talk to me while in handcuffs. I sat frozen.

"Stacy has this theory about what happened to your sister." He leaned forward and I felt myself leaning back, though he didn't appear to notice. "It ain't necessarily good, but it ain't the worst, either. That little derringer I just found out about tonight . . . We'll talk about my feelings on that later. Stacy said that after she got it, she couldn't stand herself until she tried to fire it once. So she secretly took it down to the south end, where the jetty is, and she loaded up the chambers and fired it once when nobody was around. She said the barrel is slightly bent. She said the gun went off when she fired it, but the bullet only travels about twelve feet, and she found it on top of the sand. It didn't even get enough crank to dig itself a hole."

"Stacy fired the gun?" I muttered, not getting it. I just got a flash of how somebody ought to say something before the night was over that didn't make Stacy sound atrocious.

"She's a little over the top sometimes, I'll give you that," Mr. Kearney said. "But she wouldn't shoot at nobody, and don't miss the point: *The gun ain't shootable.* I mean, it'll go off, but the bullet don't travel. In other words, whoever fired it—whether they meant to hit your sister or not— they didn't hit her. She ain't shot."

My head spun. If he was telling the truth, then the "little hole" Stern said he saw in the sweatshirt was a barnacle bite. And why the hell didn't Stacy tell me at the yacht club that the gun was defective? Maybe she figured her word was worth less than zero around here—not that the whole thing mattered as much as Mr. Kearney seemed to think.

"Sorry, but I don't feel better," I muttered back. "My sister fell three stories into a riptide because of the very presence of that gun—"

"She *dove.* Stacy says she dove. D'you hear a splash?"

The ill-fated nonsplash. At 4:34—I glanced at my watch—I wondered if we'd all been taking stupid pills . . . listening to too many pier spook stories.

"No," I confessed, embarrassed, but he laid it out anyway.

"What does that tell you? What does a clean dive sound like when there's swells coming under a pier?"

I said nothing, feeling a combination of retarded and irritated. I couldn't understand why Stacy would be having this long conversation with the guy who'd turned her life on its head, to put it mildly. *Can she really have memory loss at times?*

"Stacy said your sister's been wanting to try that dive since she could walk and talk. She said she's a good enough diver to try it if she thought she had to . . . and airy enough to forget there's a hurricane four hundred miles east, sending its hells into the riptides."

He was probably right on both counts, which made me more irritated. I looked him over, vaguely aware of this feeling that I was talking to a complete stranger. Mr. Kearney's voice was the same, but he looked very different than the last time I'd seen him, which had to have been a year ago. He'd dropped maybe forty pounds. He was shaved, and his hair was cut nice. For once he was wearing a button-down shirt instead of the PIT BULLS ARE BETTER THAN POODLES T-shirt I'd never seen him without. He had a scalded look around his collar, like men get when they've cleaned up after working outside, but he didn't look like an oversized dog-dump. He'd have passed for a white-collar professional if he'd kept his mouth shut.

"Stacy said two pretty good swells rolled in after your sister went over. If she had the sense to stay on top of the water, she probably didn't get nailed by the pilings, and she'd have gotten taken out to the down-seas in a rip. She's swimming in from the down-seas—slowly—trying to find her way in between rips. That's what Stacy hopes."

That's what everyone hoped. I did get the news flash that because Stacy had so many problems of her own, it seemed rather unselfish that she would be out looking for Casey. And here was this guy sitting in handcuffs, watching me dead-on, while he was about to be charged with god-knows-what-it's-called. I felt like I should hate him more than I suddenly hated him—if that makes sense. Not much was making sense.

"You're saying my sister dove because she thought she was being shot at."

"Yeah. That's what Stacy said."

"So who shot at her?"

"Well . . ." He sat up with a disgusted laugh. "That's the sixty-four-thousand-dollar question, ain't it? All I knows is . . . my daughter comes to us all in hysterics around mid-night, saying she's about to be charged with murder. She was bawling about swells and riptides and how it's her fault because of the gun belonging to her." He spun his head and glared at Lutz. "Me and my boys, we're all, 'What gun? Where's the gun now?' She don't know. She said she never saw it up on the pier, but she's assuming it's either hers or it's another gun that belongs to some spook . . . I don't pay no attention to no spook stories. It's hers. Bloody Christmas . . . So my big boy, Richie, says to me, 'What the hell have we been waiting for? We don't even own a couch. What furniture we've got is all rental. So let's go—*now.*'"

"You were going back to Connecticut?" Lutz asked. "To hide Stacy?"

A lot didn't make sense still, but I thought, *Damn, what a predicament for Stacy: Get devoured by your friends and arrested by the police, or risk an escape with your disgusting old man.* Maybe Mr. Kearney spiffed up so he wouldn't gross her out. Who knew.

He responded to Lutz, "Did I say yet I was answering *your* questions? I just wanna help the kid." He looked me up and down again. "My daughter likes him, all right? His sister's missing."

The silence was long, and I realized he was waiting for me to ask *my* questions. Just to be a prick I almost said, *So you were going to Connecticut to hide Stacy?* But I held on to it.

"So you don't know who fired the gun."

"She didn't tell me that part."

"How the hell could she not tell you *that* part?" I demanded. "That's seventy-five percent of it."

His answer really chilled me. "Stacy tells what she wants to tell. She holds on to what she wants to. If she's an expert on anything, it's how to tell the *what* and hold on to the *who* when somebody's guilty of something. I'd say it's almost second nature to her to protect people who are guilty."

He swallowed. The silence hung so thick, I thought for a minute we were getting a confession on the spot. But he went on with what almost sounded like nonsense, looking dead at me. "I got a lot of time on my hands in the winters, kid. Grass don't grow much after October, so you know what I do? I whittle. I make picture frames, and I had all these whittled picture frames of my kids all over me and Sam's bedroom. I made one a couple years back, and Stacy snatched it from me, all, 'You don't need another of those, silly,' which is her way of saying, 'Thanks, I'll take that.' It was a little one. So I seen it a couple weeks later. Fell out of her handbag. Had a picture in it of you and her taken out at the mall early on in high school. You remember that picture?"

I didn't. "Sort of."

"You were clowning around in front of Macy's. Anyway, that ain't the only picture of you she had, by far. So in her not-talking-about-it way, she's made me feel sort of like I've known you well. And being that you've been the center of a lot of attention tonight, I don't suppose you've missed any juicy gossip."

I didn't contradict him, but starting with Billy Nast and ending with hiding out by the questioning room, I hadn't been the center of activity. But I could see where he was going. He didn't say the word *pregnant*. I didn't say anything. I shifted uncomfortably, realizing he'd read the truth in my eyes.

He turned to Lutz. "Don't jump too fast or too far,

Lutzie. Don't go arresting me yet. You'll be sadly disappointed once the facts come in."

You could have heard a feather hit the floor.

"I'm not jumping fast." Lutz's voice sounded devoid of anything, even suspicion. I wondered how he could do that. Was he starting to think it was Stern again? Even if he did, he let Mr. Kearney go on.

"I'm going to tell you all a story. *One* story, because then I get my one phone call, and then I'm getting out of here. And kid, here is one story you need to hear that you will never hear from Stacy. Because it has to do with people, and my Stacy, she can't talk about people."

I got that same sickening ring-of-truth feeling, as when Stern had asked, "When did you ever get a straight answer out of Stacy?" Stacy talked about cars and weather and sports scores—in fact, some days she rarely shut up—but it's your thoughts about *people* that bring you closer to someone. Stacy never said a good—or a bad—word about anyone, I realized. It's like people had all the importance of sand by the sea as far as her talking went. Her actions said otherwise, but I thought that was a very dead-on statement her father had just made. I sat frozen because I was this combination of intrigued and appalled at myself for being intrigued by this guy.

"It has to do with why we came back here. Me and Stacy's mom had money problems, I ain't denying that. But we were okay . . . happy as most couples, probably a lot of it was because my boys weren't college material. But it was looking like Stacy was, and the missus got this idea in her head that we try things her parents' way for once—we make up to them so we give Stacy a chance. With me in charge of it, Stacy'd have ended up at some community college for two years and that's it.

"Me, I couldn't stand the DeWinters from day one. They used to make Sam crazy, and I realized that two seconds into the first time I talked to her. But she threatened to divorce me if I didn't do like they said and come live with them until we could get enough cash together for our own place near them. I never had my stones so much in other people's pockets, but I ain't got nothing if I don't have my family.

"But the biggest part wasn't the hell of living with your in-laws. It was watching my wife turn from seminormal into a vegetative state—and I don't mean by *seminormal* that Sam wasn't my best friend. She just was always prone to headaches and these little . . . I called them mental attacks, when she thought people were trying to break in, or one of the kids was gonna get stolen, or she was dying of cancer. After we moved here? It got worse. Not only that kind of stuff, but she'd wake up screaming from these nightmares, and she could never tell me what they were about. Before a year was up she was so doped on Valium she didn't know me half the time, and when she did it was like she was a zombie.

"I ain't no shrink, but I ain't so very stupid. All these questions I'd had over the years, they started backing up on me until they weren't just questions. They were obsessions—like, I had to know the answers. Like, how is it Samantha DeWinter could fall in love with *me*, when she could have had any stinking rich Harvard-type guy on the island back then? Why'd she agree to get married at seventeen? Why was she always getting headaches and freaking out, and then being fine again? After we moved here, *what in God Almighty's name was going on?* She'd wake up screaming with these nightmares, and I'd be all, 'Sam! What'd you dream?' And the only answer I could get was, 'I remember!'

"You got any idea where I'm going with this, kid?"

"No . . ."

He turned toward Lutz. "I bet you do, don't you?"

Lutz was trying to look blank, but it wasn't working so well. For one, his jaw dangled. Drew cleared his throat, which brought Mr. Kearney's gaze back around to me.

"Kid, you're important to my daughter, so you're important to me, too," he said like a broken record. "And you'll hear the truth someday soon, anyway. My wife, she wasn't *dreaming* . . . she was *remembering*. Being in the house brought some things back to her that you wouldn't be able to believe that a person could ever forget."

Lutz put a hand toward me, saying, "A paternity test will tell." He wanted me to get up and leave, as if Drew and I were too naive to hear this sort of thing. Maybe I was, but I didn't want to move.

Mr. Kearney just laughed in disgust and said, "You cops, you always have to have your evidence. Even if common sense tells you the truth. You ain't gonna keep me here in handcuffs until you've got that kind of evidence. Get my cell phone out of Stacy's car. Call my boys. Ask them where Stacy's been living for the past two months. She's been living with us. Now, why might that be?"

"I'd rather hear that from Stacy," Lutz said.

"Hear it from whichever of my children you want! But you probably heard some story that I got thrown out of DeWinter's house after he found me outside Stacy's room one night. Isn't that what flies through your little gossip channels? Being that nobody would ever believe me, and I couldn't prove nothing—not even to myself—I didn't add my own info to that trash heap. But let me ask you a question: What in the hell was Clifford DeWinter doing outside my daughter's bedroom in the middle of the night, to find me outside her bedroom? Where I'd been suspiciously keeping watch for weeks?"

I couldn't decide where the gross ache was coming from—my head or my stomach—or whether it was late or early . . . My watch floated in front of me automatically. 5:07. I just shot up out of the chair. It was gut instinct moving me, because I did not have any sense left to think with.

"Gotta take a leak . . . ," I said, but after I walked casually back to the rest room, I shot out the front door and sprinted the block and a half to the beach. Two girls in white-hooded sweatshirts . . . I kept seeing them both in my mind, and I couldn't tell which was my sister and which was Stacy, but suddenly they were equally important to me.

One might still be out in the water—the other was carrying some evil spawn, and if I was very, very lucky, she wasn't out there in the water by now, too.

I ran over the dune shouting, *"Casey! Stacy! Casey! Stacy!"*

I realized the only way to find my sister might be to brush up against her when I was knee-deep in surf. I was ready for anything now that I'd got through the ending of Stacy's horrific tale, the ending that I'd begged Drew for— the one that I would never have guessed.

13

High tide had been around midnight, and now it was dead low. The beach was a vast black canyon, with only little moving neon lines far off, where waves crashed at the ebb of the tide. I ran into the waves without stopping and waded out into the water up to my thighs. The thought of something clothed bumping me kept my scalp crawling, but there was some overwhelming sense of duty to this. The water was bathtub temperature, and I wished it were cold to keep me sane and sober.

If you've lived here long enough, somebody could blindfold you and stick just your feet in the water up to your ankles, and you'd be able to tell whether the tide is coming in or going out. It had just started to come in. *Between now and noon . . . this is when bodies wash up.*

I looked toward the eastern horizon, where the blotch of dark gray against black looked wider, and I knew that as dark as it was now, the sun would start showing up within half an hour. My eyes got a little more accustomed to the dark, and I strained them, forcing myself to check for something pitch-black on the now gray-black surf lines.

"Casey!" I screamed, then "—asey! —asey!" figuring I was screaming to either girl. But there was no response except the surf, which had calmed somewhat, I realized. The storm at sea must have stopped its ranting . . . maybe had fizzled down over Greenland. The ocean moaned like usual, but it was no longer booming.

"Casey?" I meant for it to come out louder, but suddenly I was having black breezes like crazy. A thousand eyes watched me from behind, from the sides and above, laughing, whispering about dead spooks and child molesters. The island was inside out . . . bad was good, good was bad, and people who were best friends turned on each other. Secrets were screaming in the black breezes. The questioning room had given me and Drew some opportunity to play God in a way—hearing people's inner thoughts, like they were being shouted from the rooftops. You could blow up, knowing what God knows. Out there in the black I felt small and petrified, certain I was about to bump into my sister's body. My toes caught on a piece of seaweed, and I all but jumped out of my skin before realizing it wasn't hair. I stubbed my toe on a jetty rock and decided maybe this walking in the water was no good.

Dragging myself in to shore and huffing, I caught sight of a long ragged hunk of inky blackness up ahead in what appeared as black-gray air. Out here all alone, the pier took on strange dimensions. I did automatically what I used to do while driving with my dad, and we would name shapes we'd see in the clouds. Every piling looked like the barrel of a gun to me. The clusters of burned-out building frames on top looked like skeleton fingers reaching for the dark sky, but unable to straighten. Rigor mortis had set in.

Something kept me from screaming my sister's name again—maybe some strange certainty that I was about to see Eddie Van Doren . . . *And why shouldn't I? If Mr. Kearney turns out to be a good father, and Mr. DeWinter a monster, why is it weird to think spooks are real? Nothing is too weird, if that's the case.*

"Casey . . ." I tried, but her name was stuck in my throat while the worst black breeze yet laced its fingers around my neck and squeezed. I had never been down here alone before at night, I realized. At least not after ten at night, when I'd walk back from a friend's with little on my mind but our dinky problems. *Navel Academy, shit. What made me ever think that was so important?*

I watched the skeleton fingers on the pier, waiting for something to move. It almost seemed impossible to me that I *wouldn't* see Van Doren dashing from one black shape to the next, trying to stay invisible, trying to lure me up there where he could—

When I saw a body dart quickly from one burned-out

shell to the next, I thought my eyes had tricked me. I stopped and watched again. Nothing moved this time, but the outline of a head and legs had been unmistakable, replaying in my mind several times. It looked like the body was missing. *He's just a head . . . shot himself in the head and now . . .*

Some crumbs of sanity sprinkled down from heaven as the head reappeared, sunk into the blackness, and then all was still. The missing body could be a white sweatshirt. *Stacy?*

As I got closer I noticed long tails of neon blowing slightly in the breeze at the base of the pier. Crime-scene tape, no question, and a cop car was parked under the streetlights at the end of Pier Drive. I stopped and let the darkness be my cover until I could decide where the cop was. It was too dark to see anything moving down there, and I wondered how Stacy had got up above without being seen.

I don't know how long I stood there letting the predawn black make me as invisible as the cop. But finally I heard my name being called from the street. I saw Drew standing beside the cop car under the streetlight, calling with his hands cupped. He looked frantic. Drew wasn't Mr. Deep Thinker, but he's got a good gauge for people—especially me. He knew that story from Mr. Kearney would turn me into a lunatic, and he didn't want me to be alone. I couldn't move, though, couldn't ease his worries. I had a chance to use his worries to my advantage, if I could just keep still.

I watched as the darkness shifted in one spot right under the pier, and a shadow moved toward the car. Drew had got the cop's attention, and he probably would keep the guy busy for a few minutes there by the car. Once I saw the officer move into the light, I made a run for the climbing mounts.

One good thing about low tide is that the exposed sand is as hard as concrete. I had to make sure to take very even steps toward the mounts and felt confident I hadn't left any footprints. I wasn't the first person to do this, I realized, as I climbed up quickly and steadily. The mounts had wet beach grit on them. *Stacy.*

My nerve always came back to me with the sun, and it was coming so quickly now that the whole eastern sky was grayish black. I had a white T-shirt on, which would make me easier to spot. I thought of ripping it off just in case another cop was around, but instead, I crawled forward to the part of the pier where the planking didn't creak and wasn't strewn with scorched holes and rotting wood. I couldn't see anything at first, but when I got toward the end, I could see the outline of a girl in a white sweatshirt, leaning against the back of the Saltwater Taffy Shoppe's scorched shell. I crawled around to Stacy, watching her stare mournfully out to sea.

She turned her head just as I came up. Anybody else probably would have jumped a little. She just looked back to sea again and said, "Scare the shit out of me, why don't you, Carmody? Keep quiet. Beach is strewn with cops."

I pulled myself around, keeping low to the planking, until I was half sitting, half lying like she was, just beside her. She was bringing something pretty big out from under her sweatshirt. It was too big to fit in the pocket and looked like it had been stashed underneath somehow.

"What've you got?" I demanded in a whisper.

She stuck them to her face. "Night vision goggles. First experimental issue, Vietnam, nineteen seventy. Only a handful of officers got them in that war. They were my grandfather's."

She said "my grandfather's" so easily I had to stare at her. She sure had a way of hiding her little hells. The way she looked through them so firmly, I had to speak.

"Stacy . . . you shouldn't be up here doing this."

She pretended she didn't hear me and let off some privacy vibe. I knew her problems, and I gathered she knew I knew them, but truths that refused to be spoken dangled in the dark air. It was the stuff I imagined she had never talked about with people—even Alisa. Stacy had only tried to lead Alisa astray with some confused story about not remembering what had happened to her—or maybe she *didn't* entirely remember. I was clueless.

"You . . . break into the museum?" I asked. I remembered seeing night vision goggles in the glass case. I'd been intrigued by them as a kid.

"Wasn't hard," she confirmed. "My grandmother has a pass key. I've had a copy for years. I like to go down there after closing and play with the swords. In a past life I think

I was a great fencer. Lately I've got this love/hate thing with weapons."

I cringed a little, glad she'd said that to me and not the cops, being that I felt I knew her slightly better. Slightly.

I couldn't stand being left in the dark. "Let me have a turn."

She kept them to her face for another thirty seconds, finally muttering, "I've got this theory, and I hope it's right," as she handed them over.

"You think Casey dove"—I stuck the goggles to my face—"because she saw someone shooting at her, and she was afraid the next shot would hit her."

"Damn, Carmody. You aren't so stupid after all."

The glasses were amazing. The water looked white. The whitecaps looked black. Anything bobbing around looked blackish red. I saw only one little piece of driftwood, but I saw it perfectly clearly.

"I actually didn't come up with that on my own," I muttered. "Been at the police station all night, hearing the yada, yada . . ."

But *she* had thought of it. I didn't see how, except through years of practice, thinking under stress. "I'm sure Lutz got his share of goop tonight," she said. "I was hoping somebody told the same thing I saw, being that I sure as hell wasn't going down there without being forced. I was a setup waiting to happen."

I couldn't deny that at all. "What did you see?"

She took the glasses back and scanned the sea as she talked. "It got pretty dark when the cloud crossed the moon, but I'd just been talking to Brin and Jon and Ronny about how Casey stuck out like a sore thumb in that sweatshirt. Shot went off—most people thought it was a firecracker, except I was very sure it wasn't. I'd heard the sound before . . . once."

She didn't mention firing the thing down at the jetty, but I remembered her father had said that. She went on, "I knew Casey wasn't shot, but the way she stumbled backward in amazement, it looked totally like—*tra-la*—she saw that someone had been aiming right for her. The moon had come back out, and I think she saw who it was. I think she was *laughing* in amazement. She fell *forward*, not backward. I think she saw Stern in the ticket booth shooting at her. By the time I looked the little window was empty, but I could have sworn somebody had just stepped back. I'd seen Stern go in there, and I figured it was him anyway. As for Casey, she took a chance. She figured the next shot might hit her, and . . . what might a diver do in a situation that out of hand?"

"Why would Mark shoot at Casey?" I asked, feeling ready to hear anything. "He seemed . . . kind of hot on her. And while he's turning into another island idiot, I wouldn't peg him as, you know . . . a natural-born killer."

She simply searched the seas, and I remembered her father's words—she can't talk about people. I had asked her to make a value judgment about someone, about whether

Mark had killer instinct, and I sensed the question simply fell away from her ears. Too tough—like maybe she didn't understand people at all. Maybe she'd become too confused about why people do the things they do.

"I hear, um . . . he asked you to go back with him tonight," I egged her on, thinking that was probably the true version, not that she'd asked him.

She muttered from under the glasses, "I told him I ought to shoot his ass."

"Shoot him?" I parroted.

"I wish I hadn't said that. He'd all but forgotten about my little gun up until that point. I reminded him. He had to go and take it, horse around with it."

"He broke into your grandfather's desk?"

She shrugged. "He must have. My grandmother's had a spare key since forever, afraid my grandfather would kick over from a heart attack and no one would know where the key was, or who was next in line to get all his charity checks. He kept all that paperwork in there, plus a couple hundred dollars in cash. When we were going out, me and Mark used to break into the desk all the time, just for ten bucks here and there. Dairy Queen money, stuff like that. The first reason Mark-the-Shark gave me for coming over tonight was that his car was busted and he wanted a loan to fix it."

The glasses made a clicking noise as she adjusted them and stared through intently. I remembered Mark saying he'd gone over to perk up the grandparents. This sounded a lot more like the Mark I knew.

"D'you tell him to go to hell?" I egged her further.

"I used to have this credit card . . . but I don't have it anymore," she said evasively. I could imagine her cutting it into a million pieces after she couldn't use it to pay for a shrink. It must have been crazy to have every purchase show up as an e-mail to her grandfather, the Tormentor. I said nothing.

She went on after a minute, "So I caught Mark in my grandfather's office while he was supposed to be in the bathroom, but I didn't say anything." She singsonged too casually, though her voice was tight, "'Yeah, yeah, rip off Stacy; if you can't get whatever you need in life some other way, there's always Stacy. She's a sport. She'll cover for you . . .'"

She adjusted the glasses again, and her voice went back to normal. "Anyway, I'm sure that's when he got the gun, looking back on it. He'd wanted to fool with it so many times. He couldn't control himself finally. Or maybe his car repair was more expensive than whatever money was in there, and he figured he'd sell it."

"Skank." I breathed. She still hadn't said why he would shoot at my sister, though I remembered a handgun assembly at school once. The cops running it said it's a little different when a kid has a gun than when a grown-up has one. All the kid needs to be is a little pissed off.

"What was he mad at Casey about?" I tried.

"You mean . . . when he shot at her? He wasn't mad at her." She readjusted the focus wheels a few times. Her lips turned to jelly, and she started that swallowing thing like she'd done last night.

"He was pissed at *me*," she said, craning her neck to the left of the pier. "Come on, Casey. Where the fuck—"

She sighed, and I let her regain some composure while waiting on pins and needles. Maybe the silence got to her. "Alisa, bless her sweet, trusting, and confused heart, just told him . . . this serious problem that I have."

"Your pregnancy."

She kept clicking the glasses, to readjust the light level, I guess. You'd think I hadn't just said the word out loud. Still, I figured she realized that I already knew—being that I'd pulled a don't-smoke-now routine on her at the yacht club. I decided I needed to know.

"He was aiming for *you*?"

"He thought he was. It got really dark." She took the glasses away from her eyes to look at me, then reached down and grabbed a big mitt of her white sweatshirt. *He had thought Casey was Stacy.*

"So he shoots his own girlfriend, thinking it's me. He'd called me a slut a few minutes earlier. Excuse me, I just wasn't in the mood. I should have just shoved him over the side and rid us all of a blood-sucking leech. I ought to have realized at some point that to control my mouth is a good thing, but . . . God forgive me of all my shortcomings." She handed me the glasses, smirking, and did the sign of the cross on herself with her thumb. "I decided to play with his head. He'd just ripped off my grandfather and left me to explain. I knew it, so I told him I'd have my family drum up some false paternity test, and he'd better get a job, because he'd be paying for the rest of his life. It was some bullshit. I never expected he would believe me."

Maybe it was a number of things . . . thinking she had cheated on him, thinking he might end up paying for a kid that wasn't his, plus that stuff from the school assembly—you don't need to be a natural-born killer if a gun is right there in your hand.

I could see the sun rising, a small streak of red on the horizon, and I thought of asking if she should be looking straight at it. She didn't seem to notice it.

"I think he threw the damn thing over the side afterward," she mumbled. "Barrel was bent anyway. He didn't hit her, but I just thought, *You know what, Stacy? Don't say a blessed word. Anything you say can—and will—be held against you.*"

"That was pretty smart." I looked through the glasses carefully, flinching when I'd see little bits of matter rolling in the surf, but it was never anything bigger than a chunk of seaweed. I didn't think we would find my sister with these glasses. It would be too lucky, and also, Crazy Addy's voice still sang out to me: *She is not in the water! . . .* Maybe I'd got my first experiences with unpredictable endings tonight, but I figured Casey was somewhere I would never guess . . . if she was still with us.

I jerked the light meter around, jumping away from those worst of thoughts one more time. I hadn't let myself

think them for more than a few seconds all night. That denial thing inside you can be your best friend in a situation like this. It keeps your pain at bay until you absolutely need it. It struck me as weird: My sister's problems were keeping Stacy from focusing too much on her own problems. Stacy's problems had been keeping me from focusing too closely on my sister. I wondered why someone didn't bottle "Helping Others" and try to sell it for a million bucks.

I could feel Stacy watching me. Her voice came through. "Last night when Bill Nast was talking about all the cool stuff he did at Purdue, I was wishing I was him. Weren't you?"

I tried for one last scan of the water, but the glasses fell away from my face and clunked me on the chest. It was the closest Stacy had come to admitting she was very unhappy, but I was caught up in another thing, too: She couldn't have known what I was talking about with Nast—unless she had been standing right there with us. I remembered feeling that outstanding black breeze behind me, the one so big I was afraid to spin for fear of Nast thinking I was an idiot.

"Oh my god." I shut my eyes. I was an idiot, for *not* having turned. I could have given Stacy an alibi. I could have prevented almost all the talk at the police station. "You were standing right there when the gun went off—right behind me—weren't you?"

With a few rays of daylight, I could see victory in her eyes. She had wanted me to know where she was—that's why she'd mentioned it. But she didn't say that.

"Well? Weren't you wishing you were Bill?"

"Yeah. Very much so," I said. "He knows who he is and what he wants."

I wanted to apologize to her, but I sensed doing so would only make her tense up. I remembered her face at the yacht club earlier, when I'd asked her where she was when the gun went off. No wonder she'd looked hurt. All I'd been thinking about was myself and the Naval Academy . . . *all summer.* She could have called me a selfish little shit, but she'd just walked off in her calm, classic way.

She took the glasses back. "You'll find your way, Carmody. You always do."

It sounded ominously like she thought she would not find *her* way. I wondered about this pregnancy until I could feel my own lower middle starting to burn and churn. *How can she stand it?* And I was wondering about this gun, why she'd bought it . . . if not for protection, maybe to flamboyantly stick it in her grandfather's face after having it under her pillow while sleeping.

There really was no way to know, because I was not going to ask. But my mind took me on travels of what might go wrong in families with people who are messed up and sneaking around about it. Half of what I thought probably came from reading my dad's books. He was drawn to hard-hitting stuff like this, and I'd read half a dozen well-researched stories with the bad guy being incestuous. The other half came from my summer of blogging with people who could tell the truth without fear of being eaten alive.

I figured Stacy and her grandfather probably had a conversation similar to what he'd said at the police station. He'd found the gun in her dresser one day. (Nobody bothered to ask Mr. DeWinter what the hell he was doing in Stacy's dresser, and I didn't want to know.) She'd probably avoided saying why she had bought it. Maybe the whole facade of her buying it as "a gift" and her grandfather taking it away from her because it was unsafe unfolded between the two of them. And maybe it happened right while her mother was in the house and her grandmother was cutting flowers just downstairs.

No wonder Stacy had scratched her mother's eyes out. No wonder her father had said he wasn't leaving without Stacy when the DeWinters offered him money to go. He'd never found the nerve to express his suspicions, and she hadn't confirmed anything to her father and brothers until last night. I imagined that prior to that, life had been like a giant play, an important exercise in "let's pretend," with actors spitting out scripted lines.

I could see it all . . . but I couldn't make any rational sense out of it. If your mother goes from slightly neurotic in Connecticut to a total Xanax queen on Mystic, why not try to discover the reasons? If your father is acting like a pig in New Jersey when he was a pretty normal guy up in Connecticut, why not demand an explanation? Why suffer all the confusion by yourself? If your grandfather breaks into your bedroom and does beyond-evil shit to you, why not just call the cops? Why rely on your own gift for melodrama

and buy a gun? Why walk through a soap opera about "Granddaughter, you shouldn't have this dangerous thing in your room" and "Grandfather, it was for your birthday"?

Somehow I *could* imagine her telling her grandfather at high noon that it was a gift for his birthday, while she'd previously imagined sticking the little barrel in his face at midnight. It didn't make sense, but my dad would write it this way. The spooks come out at midnight, causing everyone to be more dastardly, maybe. There's a daytime drama and a prime-time series, both going on in the same minds. I wondered if it were even possible that Stacy could remember at night and forget most of it during the day. People's lives can look so good on the outside and be so much dark shadow on the inside. It boggled my mind and brought more questions barreling down on me.

Like, how would she begin to tell a friend what had actually happened if she wanted to? Wasn't it worth paying Crazy Addy seventy dollars to get Alisa to leave it alone? What could Alisa say after all that?

What do I say now?

I settled on: "Your dad is perfectly safe. He's not in any trouble."

She spun her eyes to me just for a moment but then froze up again, as if I'd brought her back to herself—and away from looking for Casey. But being as I'd already gone there, I tried, "I think you should . . . go down there. Cops can help. They've been looking for you all night."

She adjusted the glasses a couple times and said in too

even a tone, "They could have picked me up anytime if they'd wanted me."

"Where were you? You told me you were going home."

"I *was* home. I've been living with my dad and my brothers."

Mr. Kearney had said so much that I'd forgotten that little bit of info. It made sense. Better safe down at the Ocean View than vulnerable in a mansion. The time flashed before me of seeing her struggling with all those pillowcases outside the Coin-Op. They don't have washers and dryers at the Ocean View. She'd flipped out on me, thinking I would start to ask questions—and the answers would be very, very complicated.

"That's good . . . it's good you were living with them," I muttered, but she ignored me, cursing and saying my sister's name in a coaxing way. She would not budge, I realized, would not unburden on me—or on anybody for that matter. She'd tried with Alisa and lost her nerve, I guessed, creating some bizarre drama with Crazy Addy. It was all a mess, mostly bottled-up smoke with just the fumes escaping. I wasn't qualified to pop the cork.

I sat in silence as the second real line of red hit the horizon. Supposedly the sun rises so fast that you can actually see it moving. But since you'd be blind if you looked directly at it, I had never done so. We sat there watching the water grow brilliant as the sky grew lighter and brighter. Beach day. Definitely. *Red sky at night, sailor's delight. Red sky at morning, sailors take warning.* Outside the sun itself,

the sky was clear, throwing a turquoise outer ring around the sun. The water was calm, the waves sounded normal, and their white neon lines looked not at all angry.

When the sun was more than a half circle on the horizon, I nudged the glasses, so Stacy's eyes broke away from them. "I don't think you need them now."

She laughed and fudged with the focus. "Duh. They work as regular field glasses, too."

"You're kidding. Gimme." I looked through them, and the rising sun brought on some positive thoughts. "Only drowning we've ever had on Mystic was that first suicide kid. They listed him as death by drowning to try to keep down the scandal. Jesus, what was his name?" I was too sleep deprived to pull it up.

"Kenny *Fife,*" she said with emphasis, then chuckled. "I got here later than you. All the stories stuck with me. I really . . . loved living here that first year."

I didn't pull the glasses away, afraid the implications of what she was saying would show in my face. I wondered, *Has her life been a hell for two of three years here? Is that how long this thing has been going on?*

There were a hundred things that no outsiders could ever know. But I felt like her boyfriend now in some unexplainable way—not that I was dumb enough to think there was a near future with a girl who was going through this much. But I felt it. I wanted to be there with her until I knew she would be okay. I kept looking through the glasses,

using one hand—and I reached down with the other and took her hand.

She let me lace my fingers through hers, though there was no response. It was like holding a warm dead squid, and when I finally looked down, she was staring at our laced fingers and her eyes were filling up. She shook her head and croaked, "It's too late."

"I'm a real patient guy," I told her.

"Yeah, about the slowest mover I've ever seen." Her smile trembled as she brushed a tear off her face. "God, I thought I was the slowest mover around. What have you been waiting for, Carmody? Mother Teresa in a flowered dress?"

I'd taken girls out only a few times. I was picky. "There is a big part of me that never felt comfortable with the people we were hanging around. They're too . . ."

"What, too normal?" she said.

I smiled, amazed at her blast of insight. "I don't need a Mother Teresa, just . . . someone the likes of which I figured I wasn't going to find around here."

"Yeah, well . . ." She laughed in a way that sounded nervous, and I wondered if I should be touching her at all. She said, "Sometimes the things you search far and wide for are right under your nose."

She gazed off to the north in a dazed way, and I tried to squeeze her hand tighter—I just didn't want to let go. The urge to kiss someone had never hit me anywhere nearly this

strongly, but it just would not have worked. For whatever perverted reason, I thought of the movie *Rosemary's Baby,* with the woman carrying the Antichrist. I wondered if Stacy felt like that.

This situation was beyond fixable, beyond belief, beyond scandalous, beyond *me,* and I couldn't understand what was preventing Stacy from leaping into the surf. My sister was giving her superhuman strength, I decided, and for a second I was glad Casey went missing.

I babbled, "Stacy, I'm sorry . . . I'm sorry you were always right here, and I just had no idea how you felt or . . . what you were about."

The laugh she finally threw in didn't surprise me. Stacy laughed at everything. "Christ, the gossip must have been thick at the cop station."

My vision was blurred from tears, but not so much that I couldn't see her face turn to an outright smile—one of the few genuine ones I'd ever seen.

"Kurt, stop being romantic. You are about the dumbest shit I've ever met." With that, she brought my knuckles up to her mouth and kissed them absently. She was still gazing off into the north sea. *"The things you're looking for are right under your nose!* Turn your fool head," she hollered.

I guess not all things end in ways that you just couldn't guess. If I'd had any hope of finding my sister, it would have been by seeing her coming ashore alive, having swum in from the down-seas. The beach was now lit, but at the sun-

rise the water looked white, except for one bobbing blotch about a block off, only about thirty feet from the beach. It was not a pretty sight. The first thing that came clearly to my stunned eyes was the color red. A red blob. I wiped my eyes quickly, rising slowly to my feet in shock. The red grew more clear, despite the distance between me and the blob. *It was Casey's back.* I could barely see bluish arms moving, plodding downward in the water. But my ace swimmer sister could not lift her head, and I couldn't tell what she was floating on.

"Looks like Van Doren's Dungeon threw her a surfboard," Stacy said, pushing at me. I remembered the surf club babbling on about Tito's lost board. "Go, you moron!"

Stacy pushed me again, but as the daylight threw plenty of light on the beach, I could see not one but two cops, running toward Casey. I ran back toward the brackets, and my eyes filled up and spilled over in relief. But I was not moving as quickly as I should have been. Some invisible force was pushing back on me—like in those dreams where you're trying to run but you can't. I finally reached the brackets, took the first two down, and stopped, my face right about at Stacy's feet. I wiped my eyes and looked up. Her face was shrouded in dawn shadows, but I could have sworn her eyes were filling again.

"Go!" She kicked at my fingers. "The girl's already had one broken neck! She's your sister!"

"Listen to me. I'm coming right back." I held my grip

and just spewed my worst thought, "Don't you dare jump." I don't know what had given me the nerve, but with that the whole major cat was out of the bag. She knew I knew, and I was amazed at her calm.

She stooped down and rubbed my hair. "I promise you, I will not jump. Just go before I kick your ass down there."

I went down the brackets, these insane tears of relief pumping—insane because I'd been in denial all night. I had no idea how scared I had really been until I bawled in relief for Casey, for my parents, for myself—and for Stacy's ability to keep her wit even in the worst of situations. I ran up the beach. Casey seemed to be coming to shore maybe a block away, a span that looks like nothing on the beach, but it's a good jog if you haven't had sleep and invisible forces are pushing against you.

Just about when I was halfway there, the cops reached Casey and were pulling the board in to shore. Whistles were blowing, sirens flashed from the cop car on the street, and a police jeep broke across the dunes with lights going everywhere.

And I turned and started running back to the pier as fast as my legs could carry me.

Stacy breaking into the museum to get out night vision goggles . . . That thought was under my skin all of a sudden, and I got images of all the other stuff that was in there: big guns, war guns . . . swords, daggers . . . And why had her eyes been filling up again as I left her?

The shot rang out loud enough to tell me that it wasn't any little derringer this time. Stacy had taken something from the museum that had size and volume. To this day I don't know whether it was a good thing or a bad thing that Chief Aikerman beat me to the mounts. One cop climbed up while Chief Aikerman lay on top of me blathering—and my own yells got buried in mouthfuls of rising seawater.

 **14**

Stacy Kearney's funeral was attended by just about every-one on Mystic. The huge arrangement of yellow roses that covered the casket seemed all wrong somehow. Yellow is a lukewarm, say-nothing color. I figured her flowers should have been white peace roses, for all the peace she'd tried to keep, or flaming red for her flamboyancy, which I will miss forever.

I sometimes relive that hour in Saint Thomas Maritime Cathedral when I sat in a pew in the balcony, watching below, holding Casey's hand, glad that she'd developed a sudden love of silence.

Casey and I went through the mourners' line early, and I don't remember what I said to Stacy's mom and grand-mother, but I took one look at her dad and brothers and about busted in half. They'd been over to my house the day

after she died, understanding that I had found her and had "been with her."

So by the day of the funeral, I had all my blather out on the table, had already apologized twenty-five times for being too dumb to save her, had already listened to them tell me just as many times that it wasn't my fault. At one point a swollen-eyed Mr. Kearney said in my den, "Enough, already! Will you shut up about it?"

I loved those three guys from that moment forward. They remind me of her.

At the church they actually wanted me to stand in the receiving line—as the bereaved boyfriend—a concept that made me fall back in horror. I was not deserving and gave the truth as an excuse—I had to look after Casey. She was in a back brace, with one cracked vertebra and twenty stitches in various places, four on her face. Barnacle bites. She hadn't complained at all about stitches, the pain, or a dozen scratches on her face along with the sutures. She had insisted on coming, but if anybody tried to hug her—that could have made her scream in agony.

I was glad to take a seat with her up in the balcony, where we could sit and vegetate, and I could bawl if I wanted to, or pray if I got the urge. We watched the Marvels file through below in one unbroken line, giving pictures to Mrs. Kearney and Mrs. DeWinter, and laying "memories" in a big basket at the altar, until it overflowed into the aisle. Tennis rackets, CDs, shoes, journals . . . anything that had given Stacy a giggle lay there, and it collectively

resembled the contents of some old giant closet that had been dumped out.

I watched in kind of a daze, looking for what details left me feeling that the Marvels were just going through the motions of being Marvels—maybe without realizing themselves that they were little more than lonely, pathetic bodies wandering around. One nice detail that stands out was how no one seemed to be looking into the eyes of anyone else. Not that anyone appeared to feel treacherous or deceitful or remorseful for how she or he had treated Stacy lately—I didn't sense that.

It was something else. A lack of reliance, maybe. You search your friends' faces when you're feeling terrible things, and you need to see that your friends are in it with you. When you don't look, it's either that you don't have those feelings or you don't feel that your friends do. Either way, it was hard to watch.

Stern was the only one not there. He was in county jail, looking at eight-to-ten for attempted manslaughter, which I thought was a charitable charge. I hadn't said anything to Casey like, "I warned you about that jerk." One of the things that was making us closer, I think, was my not saying it. Another thing was the discussions we'd had all yesterday.

The tale Casey told came down pretty much like Stacy had predicted. Casey heard the shot, felt nothing, but saw Stern pointing a gun straight at her, just after she'd seen an orange crack from the corner of her eye. She had no idea that he was mistaking her for Stacy, but her flight mode

went off. She dove, thinking she was in serious danger for reasons she couldn't understand but could figure out later.

The perfect dive, yeah. Stacy was right about that. Casey cut the water so pristinely that under the pier, she was able to get out of my sweatshirt before the first swell hit her. She said that as often as she'd considered trying this dive, she had never in her wildest dreams understood the thrust of the waves under the pier. The first one spun her ten feet under, eggbeater style, then all but nailed her to one of the pilings. At ten feet down at high tide, the barnacles are about three feet thick. They're like razors, and they cut her to shreds, cut right into a vertebra, then mercifully sucked her into a rip that took her out.

The rest is a lot of ramble that was hard for her to put into words and harder for me to hear. She said there was a night surfer out there, and somewhere between the pier and the down-seas, he helped her onto a surfboard, and she lay on it in excruciating pain. She had no clue how much time had passed between when the surfer helped her and when they found Tito's surfboard. She said only that it was dark and she was weak, probably from blood loss. At one point she opened her eyes and he was gone, maybe having lost track of her in the swells . . . She knew at that point that she'd have to get herself back to shore with a back that hurt like a bitch—and without paralyzing herself. She took her time.

She wondered aloud to me whether it had been the ghost of Kenny Fife, or if it had been an angel—or just

some total moron who went surfing after dark when there was only a trickster half moon. I don't speculate on that, except to reflect on how no guy ever showed up at the police station to report that he'd helped a girl onto a surfboard and then lost her in the swells, and no dead surfer ever washed up. The bottom line is that my sister is a sadder but wiser, more realistic person.

She put her fist on my knee after we sat in the pew for a few minutes. She was utterly baked on pain pills, so she slurred. "D'you see how everyone kissed me?"

As we'd been heading up to the balcony, most of the Marvels were coming in. She'd asked them, please, not to hug on her back brace, so everybody had kissed her and told her how great she looked and how lucky they all were that she was still with us. They asked her questions about her brace, and they clucked over her a lot.

"Yeah. They were okay to you."

She blasted out her nose, "To my face. Rumor's already circulating that this is my fault somehow. My melodramatic exit off the pier caused the police to be distracted, or they might have had more time to help Stacy. Insane . . . but normal for these parts."

I wondered where she had heard that, didn't exactly care, and said nothing.

But she slurred on, "So I think I'm next in line to be the Fallen Queen."

I liked the way she giggled evilly. We'd talked about the Marvels a lot yesterday, how she'd given the crowd its famed

nickname, how a night at sea had changed her. We were both still messed up, to the point where I don't think we ever finished a sentence. We didn't really have to.

"So . . . are you expecting to stick around and accept the honor?" I mumbled.

Another little snort escaped her. "I haven't made up my mind how weird I actually want to be yet. I just know, based on what I have saved up this summer, I only have enough in my budget for four piercings. Where should I get them? All places that show, thank you. Stacy would be mad if I were, um . . . vulgar about it."

They say people get weird urges to laugh at funerals—along the lines of laughing and crying being the same release. I felt the corners of my mouth wanting to turn strangely up, but I fought off the impulse. "Just don't put a plate in your bottom lip."

She shifted. Her back had stung so bad last night, she'd slept on the couch on her stomach, with her face hanging over onto the ottoman—with just enough room between the ottoman and the couch for her nose and mouth, so she could breathe. She never complained, though. After her halo rantings, that seemed miraculous.

"Duly noted," was all she said, and we slipped into silence.

We got to see how strange it looked for something huge to be happening on the island without Mr. DeWinter being at the center of it. Because Drew and I had been the only Marvels present to hear Mr. Kearney set the whole thing straight, the funeral was a very surreal time of limbo. Mr.

DeWinter had not been arrested yet. I don't know if the cops were dotting all their *i*'s and crossing all their *t*'s, but it was three weeks until the arrest actually took place and the media storm hit. So at the funeral, the only word on the street was that he was in the hospital. Most people still thought Stern was the father.

I started to notice, as this endless line of people kept coming, that very few of them were hugging Mr. Kearney and Stacy's brothers. It pissed me off to the point that I felt the urge to stand up and announce the Whole Truth and Nothing But the Truth. I figured the arrest of Mr. DeWinter was coming—Lutz had stopped by the house and told us in confidence that testing had confirmed him as the rapist. So I just watched. Everyone hugged on Stacy's mom—the drug addict, the one-time victim, the person who probably had every reason to guess what was happening to Stacy from having lived through it herself. She probably "remembered" it all when she came back here, my dad says, and chose to lace herself up to believe it couldn't happen again.

And to everyone Mr. Kearney was still "the slug" who had looked for all the grossest jokes to tell at the famed DeWinter garden parties, until the garden parties were no more. I could see totally why he acted like such a pig. It was a protest against the well-behaved. There was something gallant about the thought that had come the closest, over the past few days, to making me smile.

And I remembered the haze of someone saying in the questioning room that pedophiles often consider their rela-

tionships sacred. What was Mr. DeWinter going to do besides quit throwing parties after the Kearneys came to live with him? Throw Mr. Kearney out and risk losing Stacy? He never threw Mr. Kearney out until he'd been caught like a cat on the prowl. I thought again of the "settlement" Mr. DeWinter had offered him to leave Mystic. I wondered if Mr. Kearney bothered at that point to call it blood money to the old man's face. He'd had no proof then of wrongdoing. It was probably another of those stunning facts that never got said.

I still freeze up and sputter over the idea of all that probably was never said—by anyone, but especially not by Mr. Kearney. My dad and I had discussed how Mr. Kearney had been in a real jam. How do you ask your daughter if her grandfather is that sort of evil? If the dad gets the nerve to ask and the daughter is too afraid or psyched-out to tell, what do you say then?

My worst thought, while watching Mrs. Kearney get hugs and Mr. Kearney get frosty handshakes, was, *Did Stacy think of my dad?* Had she thought of all the people like him who had got DeWinter money over the years—and would now get nothing if she sent his butt to jail? It would seem like an insignificant thought in comparison to her own predicament, but that's one thing my dad confirmed for me about victims like her: The ways in which they are messed up are beyond tragic. They can adopt the minds of angels to make up for their physical world being a hell.

On that note I lost it, and my crying felt like a train wreck. I was glad to be in the back with no one but my

sister, who had heard me bawl enough over the past few days to view it as normal.

The Kearney men got tired of being snubbed, I gathered. They excused themselves and five minutes later showed up beside Casey and me. We all sat together in the balcony, which, if nothing better, prevented any of the Marvels from coming up to chat with us. Except Drew.

He came up and sat with us for a while. But sensing, I think, that Casey and I needed to be left alone, he wandered downstairs. He didn't ask any questions. I was about to leave this church and begin a life in search of originality, which for months would include thoroughly disliking any person who looked too normal. But I sensed even at the service that Drew would be one mindless conformist I would always forgive, because he's got special gifts. He had stayed with me the whole night Casey was missing, and he never left me the next day until noon, when I finally crashed out on my family room floor and slept twenty-four hours straight. If you're the nicest guy in the world, you can have a whole lot of shortcomings.

I watched Alisa Cox leave after saying her good-byes to Stacy by the casket. She had the classic nerve not to cry at all. She didn't say good-bye to anyone else, and I don't know what became of her. No one on the island has seen her again, though the rumor flies that she, too, committed suicide, and the service that followed was private. Casey tells the more likely story, considering that Alisa's parents still smile smugly when seen in the supermarket but seem other-

wise reclusive. They wouldn't be smiling if their daughter died. The less popular rumor is that Alisa did her senior year at a boarding school for precocious gifted kids who want a sure deal into Harvard. Sometimes I wish I knew more.

Maybe five minutes after the Kearney men sat down beside me, I spotted Crazy Addy coming up through the mourners' line, getting ready to hug Mrs. DeWinter. I almost shot up in the pew to shout a warning at her to keep her big mouth shut. I'd been scared she would start in on some self-righteous loud trek about predicting how a girl would die at dawn. She had been right again with her predictions. But she merely hugged the family silently, then took a place in the balcony not far from us.

She looked down at Casey, and then at me. I sensed there was some recognition in Crazy Addy's tearful eyes, though she hadn't seen me at the police station, hadn't been parading herself all over the beach when Stacy died, like she had after the Van Doren debacle. I'd been in her place a couple times years ago, but so had every other teenager on Mystic, so it probably wasn't any memory that made her smile at me.

I waved and she waved back. I wished I hadn't. For whatever reason it inspired her to get up, come over, and sit down on the other side of Casey. I had the Kearneys sitting on my left, which was enough; I didn't need a drama developing to my right. I got ready to say, "Do *not* freak out my sister by telling her anything clairvoyant." But Crazy Addy seemed content just to sit there and not say anything. I got

a twitch that maybe she was just lonely. Everyone around here is lonely.

When the priest finally started in with the Lord's Prayer, I simply could not pray at first. I sat there numbly, watching the Mystic Marvels, noticing how not many of them were praying, either, and caught myself before gloating over *their* hypocrisy.

I wouldn't have had a chance, anyway. Mr. Kearney had his worst breakdown yet as he was reciting the Catholic prayers, and I don't remember who grabbed for whose hand first. But me, my sister, this row of Kearneys, and Crazy Addy held hands for those prayers, and I got the deep impression Mr. Kearney had recited them over and over and over throughout the years, looking for something—sense maybe, strength maybe, forgiveness for defaulting to playing a pig role, maybe.

Memories of Stacy claiming to be a devout Catholic shot through me—despite that she'd always been given to moments of extreme mouthiness and self-defensive outbursts—and I figured she'd followed her father's example, the only example in her life that held much meaning.

And I prayed for Stacy, maybe half *to* her, and Casey heard me, and she started praying just as loud as Mr. Kearney and his two sons.

That was the first experience in my life that made me understand religion—as much as you can "understand" religion. I was sending out words that had little to do with sense but had everything to do with communicating, with

belonging. I was in a row with two slobs; their father, who was a pig; a girl ripped to shreds by barnacles; and a woman who was probably as embarrassed by her talents as she was proud of them. And we were praying our fool heads off. And it should have looked pathetic, and it probably would have if we hadn't been in the dead back row for no one to see.

Mr. Kearney's fifteen-hundredth reciting of the Lord's Prayer hadn't managed to save his daughter, and yet he was bothering to pray it again—and something behind his lawn mower voice was making all of us say it, and to feel something that is beyond understanding. But I didn't feel pathetic. I felt like I was exactly where I belonged . . . surrounded by people who had been through the worst, the most embarrassing, the most mysterious of life's dealings, and were willing to not sell their souls to have friends.

After we said "Amen," Mr. Kearney wiped his eyes, but doing so was pointless, a major flood. He managed to say something directly to me, which I think had to do with how ridiculous we probably looked compared to people who seemed so stoically together, like the Marvels. He said with lawn mower force, "It ain't over till it's over."

I have never seen him again. I want to see him, but I'm a far cry from where he is. I think he and his sons are back in Connecticut. I'm in California now. I spend a lot of time watching an ocean where the sun sets over it instead of rising over it. But I watch every sunset that I can, and I think of Stacy every time.

I think of writing to the Kearney men, or calling, even,

but something stops me. We'd collected ourselves as best we could at the end of the service, and the oldest son, Richie, exchanged e-mail addresses with me and Casey. But some people you remember as bigger than they are, and you don't want to break that up into smaller human pieces. They haven't written to me, either, so I leave it alone.

Starting the first of August, I did a trek cross-country with nothing but a mountain bike and a thousand bucks in cashed-in college savings. I landed in Santa Monica sometime in early December. I've bused a lot of tables, learned to play the guitar, and kept blogging from my room in a little Santa Monica motel that backs up to the beach—the room I've called home all year.

Casey e-mails that my blogs have become famous on the island, along with pictures I send that she shows around. She says that I've stirred up a shit storm with former friends and wannabes, what with all my liberal hair-mess guitar playing, with motel living and my West Coast surfer-boy life. I've *wanted* to stir up storms. I want people to remember what they did to Stacy—because she was a little too flamboyant, a little too rich, a little too poor, a little too giving, a little too bratty. I love thinking of what hells people go through over someone who doesn't conform well, but who happens to be out of firing range.

Beyond that, I don't know what to say about what happened to Stacy. Would it help to run around high schools, giving speeches about not judging? Casey says that no mat-

ter where you go, there will always be Mystic Marvels, lots of people who refuse to know the difference between "good" and "the appearance of good." To most people, she says, appearances are everything. Maybe I'm pulling a cop-out, but I believe my sister. I'm not up for speeches.

My dad came out in early May, to complete a second deal with Paramount. He's got major bucks all of a sudden, and he pays for this motel room. I've refused to go east and see their new digs in the beach block, but I'm happy for them.

I was glad he came. Not only did I miss his blather about many aspects of the human condition, but I had some news that I wanted to tell him to his face. We got back to my motel from the airport, and out on the balcony I gave him a glass of two-buck-a-bottle Boone's Farm, one type of alcohol I can hack without puking, if I limit myself to one glass. I toasted the Pacific, and then him.

"I'm going to school in the fall. I've even declared a major."

He clanged glasses with me, looking hopeful. "Uh . . . med school?"

"Nuh-uh."

"Engineering?"

"Nuh-uh."

He knows me better than that. When I got scared to say, he plopped down on my beach chair, and I sat on the concrete beside him.

He drank fast, nervously. "Tell me no. Not my offspring."

I had never really thought until then how much pressure to go to the Naval Academy had come from him.

"Do you *like* peanut butter, Kurt?" he asked. "Do you want to spend fifteen years having your face smeared into the concrete? There's no politics in the writing world—I cannot pull strings for you. I cannot do it for you."

I told him I don't want to write any *bad* novels, so I needed his help.

"The only way around is through," he told me. "You'll write bad fiction for ten years. At least."

Well, I've been blogging all year, and I'm trying to side-step the "bad fiction" route with a "true story." And maybe it is still bad . . . maybe this reads like so many flashback blogs with bad transition statements and a poor attempt at cleanup. But my life on Mystic is finished, my years in high school are behind me—though I'll never stop thinking about Stacy. If nothing else, in all these words, I have a memorial to Stacy Kearney that tells as much as you can tell about somebody whose life was a mystery, an endless secret, and yet, you know you're right to love her forever.

And I guess when I'm a really good writer, I'll know how to end a story better. 'Cuz all I can think to say is, "Cheers to surf—she's another great and mysterious babe—and cheers to peace."

Peace is good, brothers and sisters.